THE Love-Shy Lord

MONA PREVEL

DIVERSIONBOOKS

Also by Mona Prevel

A Kiss for Lucy
The Dowager's Daughter
Eudcating Emily

Diversion Books
A Division of Diversion Publishing Corp.
443 Park Avenue South, Suite 1008
New York, New York 10016
www.DiversionBooks.com

For more information, email info@diversionbooks.com

First Diversion Books edition April 2014.
Print ISBN: 978-1-62681-681-7
eBook ISBN: 978-1-62681-273-4

Dedicated to my lovely granddaughters:
Amanda, Debi, Karie, and Heather.

Chapter 1

"Lady Camberly, I understand you are to be my dinner companion this evening. What an unexpected pleasure." Marcus Ridley looked up as he bowed over the titian-haired beauty's hand and gave her the merest hint of a wink.

"La, my lord. The pleasure is mine," the beautiful French émigrée replied. As she dipped him a curtsy she whispered, "Behave yourself, Marcus. I should like to be asked back."

Marcus could not blame her for that. The culinary skills of Lord and Lady Ambrose's chef were the envy of the *ton*, so upon receiving an invitation to attend one of their soirees, Marcus Ridley had accepted with alacrity.

Having the Dowager Countess of Camberly for a dinner partner was an added pleasure. The charming Celeste, whose youthful appearance belied her thirty-nine years, was not only a good friend, her daughter Althea, Countess of Camberly in her own right, was married to his younger brother, John.

"And how are the lovebirds?" he asked, once they were seated and partaking of a particularly delectable turtle soup. "Still billing and cooing, I trust?"

She laughed. "Even more so since your nephew was born. Seaview House is awash with their love. But you will see for yourself next weekend at his christening."

"Sooner than that. I shall arrive there in a couple of days. Thought I would put in an early appearance—get acquainted with my nephew and godson before he is engulfed on the weekend by visitors oohing and aahing over him."

"In that case, I shall cut my visit to London short and do likewise. I would welcome some lively conversation."

"That is a terrible responsibility to lay at my door. By

the way, who does Percy favor, the Markhams or the Ridleys? The last time I saw him it was difficult to tell. He looked like a wizened little gnome."

"Marcus! What a dreadful thing to say about my darling grandson." Her deep green eyes sparkled with mirth. "Actually, he favors neither family."

Marcus raised a brow. "Neither?"

Celeste patted her curls. "His hair is fast becoming as red and as curly as mine, so I think it is safe to presume that you are harboring a de Maligny in your midst."

Marcus raised his wine glass. "If Percival John Markham Ridley proves to be half as charming as his maternal grandmother, I think both the Markhams and the Ridleys should consider themselves most fortunate."

"La, darling, you are dangerous enough without the charm," Celeste whispered. "No wonder you are always in such a pickle with one lovelorn lady after another."

Marcus put down his spoon. "That is a low blow, especially coming from a friend," he whispered in return. "I do no more than observe the niceties of polite society, and you know it."

Celeste leaned closer. "You should have exercised more restraint in the doing when it came to young Caroline Ambrose. After all, this is her very first Season, and you are far too rich a delicacy for her to digest."

Marcus groaned. "What now? All that passed between us were the requisite how-do-you-dos."

"See for yourself. The young lady is situated directly opposite you, and her gaze has not left your face since you sat down."

Marcus made eye contact with Caroline Ambrose, and the pert little blonde batted her eyelashes at him.

"Oh, dear," Celeste murmured, "our Caroline flutters her eyelids with the rapidity of hummingbird wings. I wonder how she does that."

Marcus gave the young girl the most withering stare he could muster and then, while smiling at an elderly widow seated farther down the table, whispered to Celeste between clenched teeth. "I fail to see the humor in the situation. I was looking forward to this meal, and now I have quite lost my appetite."

"Pah!" Celeste rejoined. "A gentleman of your sophistication should not be thrown by the antics of a silly child. She is but an irritating little gnat and should be accorded the same consequence."

"One can swat a gnat Unfortunately the same cannot be said of Lady Caroline. Oh lord, she is at it again. She must create a draft sufficient to put out the candles with her ridiculous fluttering."

Celeste smiled archly. "Ah, me. The price one pays for being irresistible."

"And to think, my lady," Marcus rejoined, affecting an air of exaggerated dismay, "that I considered you to be one of the more charming ladies of the *ton*. I must have been absolutely mad."

"Serves you right. You should know better," Celeste responded cheerfully.

Their banter was interrupted by the necessity of having to stand to raise their glasses in a toast proposed by their host.

Lord Ambrose, a gentleman whose once handsome face was becoming more bejowled and red-veined with each passing day, beamed at his guests. "Ladies and gentlemen, let us raise our glasses in celebration of our victory at Badajos. And to our gallant soldiers whose bravery made it possible."

Amid a resounding chorus of "Hear, hear," Celeste and Marcus smiled at each other and sipped their wine. When they were seated once more, footmen removed their soup bowls and replaced them with servings of wonderfully fresh looking Scottish salmon.

To his relief, Lady Caroline's bad behavior notwithstanding, Marcus found his appetite was not in the least impaired, and he worked his way through the subsequent dishes and removes with the gusto the artistry of their creator deserved.

When the last morsel of food had been eaten and the final toast made, the ladies withdrew from the dining room, leaving the gentlemen to enjoy their brandy and cigars and to discuss the war being waged on the Iberian Peninsula against

Napoleon's France.

When the gentlemen joined the ladies in the withdrawing room, Marcus declined making up a foursome at a game of whist in favor of conversing with a Mrs. Baxter, a widowed friend of his mother's. He would be seeing his mother on the morrow and knew she would like to hear how her friend was faring.

He stood while exchanging pleasantries with the lady, deeming it would make it far easier to take his leave of her if he chose not to sit down. Past encounters with Mrs. Baxter had taught him that it did not always pay to tarry in her company.

"How are you getting along, Mrs. Baxter?" he enquired of the plump, gray-haired matron. "My mother is sure to ask when I see her tomorrow."

She rewarded him with a warm smile. "It is good of you to take an interest. You may tell your mother that I am in fine fettle, but have yet to forgive Mr. Baxter for attempting that jump at the Caswells' hunt the autumn of ought-nine. At his age, he should have known better."

She removed a handkerchief from her reticule and dabbed the corner of her eye.

It was now the spring of 1812. Marcus was of the opinion that forgiveness was way overdue. He leaned over her chair and gave her hand a sympathetic pat. "He is sorely missed by all his friends."

"I cannot imagine how he failed to address that jump. He was such a fine horseman."

When sober, Marcus thought.

Some who had attended the hunt on that fateful morning had told him that the worthy gentleman had partaken too freely of the stirrup cup and had been hard put to stay on his horse, much less make a jump.

"Mr. Baxter was, indeed, the finest of horsemen," he soothed.

Mrs. Baxter grasped at this. "Everyone says so." She heaved a sigh. "I suppose it is not for mere mortals to question the ways of the Lord."

Suddenly she clutched Marcus's sleeve, her air of martyrdom

giving way to an avid interest in the doings on the other side of the room.

"I declare. Elizabeth Ambrose should take Caroline over her knee and whip some sense into her. That little baggage is ogling you with the subtlety of a street strumpet."

Marcus was used to Mrs. Baxter's disconcerting penchant for blurting out whatever popped into her head, so without batting an eye he replied, "Her time and energy could be put to better use. I have no interest in Bath misses."

Mrs. Baxter gave him a reproving look. "Much to your mother's dismay. What other choice is there for a young man in your position, pray tell? I can hardly see you dusting off an old maid and taking her to wife. I have seen you in the company of far too many beautiful jades to believe you would settle for an antidote." This remark was made with a pointed look in Celeste's direction.

Such an outburst was outrageous even for Mrs. Baxter. Besides, lumping Celeste Markham among his conquests did the lady a great injustice. Nothing untoward had ever taken place between them.

Marcus decided to take his leave of her. Too many variations on the same theme had passed his mother's lips for him to suffer more of the same from her bosom friend.

He accorded her a parting bow. "Conversing with you is always a delight, dear lady. I shall be sure to tell my mother how well you are looking."

From the corner of his eye, he saw Caroline coming toward him, the rustle of the yellow taffeta ruffle on the hem of her white dress proclaiming her intent to the others in the room.

Marcus quickly veered in Lady Ambrose's direction, presuming that even a goose brain such as Caroline was hardly likely to misbehave in front of her mother.

Lady Ambrose had just prevailed upon a Miss Minns, a young spinster noted for her plain features and an extraordinary talent for playing the pianoforte, to execute some Mozart pieces for her guests. Lady Ambrose signaled for Marcus to sit beside her during the performance.

As the purity and grace of Mozart's music filled the room, the guests ceased their chatter and listened in awe.

Although Miss Minns lacked both beauty and consequence, it was generally agreed that as long as her fingers remained supple enough to play the pianoforte, she would not lack for dinner invitations to the finest establishments of the *ton*.

During a particularly poignant passage, Marcus was startled by the sensation of a slight pressure on the back of his hand. He glanced down to see that his hostess's gloved fingertips had come to rest there.

He gave Lady Ambrose a quizzical look and she responded with an upswept glance through fluttering lashes. Evidently Caroline had come naturally by the silly habit. Marcus resigned himself to having to discourage yet one more amorous matron as tactfully as possible.

Fortunately, Miss Minns chose that moment to come to the end of her performance, so Marcus stood up and started a round of enthusiastic applause that was quickly taken up by the rest of the guests.

When the applause had died down, and Miss Minns, her face pink with pleasure, had taken her final curtsy, Marcus took his leave of everyone, using his impending journey on the following morning as an excuse.

He made his escape, relieved to have come through the evening relatively unscathed. It was all very well for Celeste to tease him about his irresistible charm, but Marcus was tired of having females of all ages and from all walks of life flirting with him at every turn, remarking as to how tall and how handsome he was.

When told by lovesick females that his hair was not merely dark but black as ravens' wings and that his eyes were not just blue but like the depths of mountain tarns or twilit skies, Marcus cringed.

More than one young man in his circle of friends confessed to him that if such a thing were possible, he would sell his soul to the devil to be in Marcus's shoes. In each case, Marcus thought that his friends should be more circumspect when it came to making wishes. The adulation of the opposite sex merely gave him the feeling of being the prey at a hunt that never ended.

He breathed a sigh of relief when his carriage drew up under the porte cochere. Viewing the steady downpour of an April rain, he was exceedingly glad that he had chosen it over the curricle as a means of transport

A footman held the door open for him and, once he was settled, snapped it closed. The night air was damp and bone chilling, and Marcus grabbed a fur lap robe lying on the carriage floor, intending to avail himself of its warmth.

To his surprise, the lap robe offered resistance. With an extra tug, he jerked it aside to reveal a huddled form on the floor. The rustle of taffeta and a flash of yellow amid a pool of white silk clearly illuminated by the torches blazing under the porte cochere gave Marcus cause to groan.

He hauled Caroline to her feet and unceremoniously deposited her on the seat facing him.

"Explain yourself, young lady. Although what you could possibly say that would mitigate your disgraceful behavior is beyond me." This delivery was punctuated by a forbidding look.

Caroline clutched her bosom. "La, Lord Ridley, you are so masterful when you are angry, I fear I shall swoon."

"Nonsense. I shall have my man drive us around to the shrubbery, where you will oblige me by making a discreet exit from this carriage and returning to the bosom of your family before everyone discovers what a silly little pea-goose you are."

Caroline's lower lip jutted forward. "You cannot make me. I am deeply, passionately in love with you, and you have to love me back. You just *have to.*" Tears glistened on her cheeks.

Marcus had thought to put her out of the carriage on reaching the shrubbery with or without her consent, but at the sight of her tears could not bring himself to do so. Instead, he removed a handkerchief from his coat pocket and handed it to her.

"Without a doubt, you are a thoroughly delightful, lovable young thing, and I am flattered by your attention," Marcus said, almost choking on the words. "I am sure that one day you will meet your true love and be glad that I did not take advantage of your innocence."

Caroline eyed him warily. "T-take advantage?"

"But of course. Everyone knows that I absolutely refuse to be leg-shackled."

"But I can *make* you love me. I *know* I can."

Marcus smiled and patted her cheek. "Only someone incredibly young and romantic could harbor such an illusion. Now, Caroline, I am going to instruct my driver to drop you off at the shrubbery, and I want you to return to the withdrawing room as quickly as possible."

Caroline responded with a scowl.

Marcus felt his patience running out. "You *do* wish to marry some day, do you not?"

"I wish to marry you."

"You are not the first young lady to hide in my carriage thinking I would be honor bound to save her reputation with an offer of marriage. Quite a few have done so, but I have not obliged them. Most of the misguided creatures have gone on to marry others, but if you do not do as I say, I am afraid, Caroline dear, that your reputation will be ruined and no gentleman of any consequence will offer for you."

Caroline looked at him with loathing. "Let me out of here, you horrid, horrid, man. I would not marry you if you were to get down on your knees and beg me."

Marcus smiled. "Brava, Caroline, that's the spirit."

Caroline raised her chin. "It is *Lady* Caroline to you, sir."

Marcus was impressed. It seemed that Caroline Ambrose had left her childhood behind in a matter of minutes. He stuck his head out of the window and said to his coachman, "You may proceed, Grimes. Just be sure to stop for a moment when you round the shrubberies. A young *lady* wishes to alight"

"Again? Criminy, your lordship, I am sorry about that."

As Marcus rode his large black gelding, Achilles, to Surrey the following morning to visit his parents, the Earl and Countess of Fairfax, try as he might he could not help but think of the events that had taken place at the Ambroses' soiree the previous evening. Each scene replaced yet another like the ever-changing patterns of a kaleidoscope.

He recalled Celeste likening Caroline to a gnat, and the expression brought to mind another girl to whom he and his brother John had given the same nickname. A very little girl who would chase after them all over the grounds at Fairfax on her short legs, calling out, "Rissa go too."

He smiled as he thought of the red-haired, freckle-faced Clarissa, the daughter of his father's steward, Edwin Carter. Even as a boy, he could not fathom how the tall, sedate Mr. Carter could have fathered such a boisterous little girl.

His thoughts then turned to his conversation with Mrs. Baxter. It had been so unjust of her to include Celeste in his list of paramours on the basis of idle rumors. His usually generous mouth compressed with outrage on the slur perpetrated on the good name of a friend.

His relationship with Celeste had led most members of the *ton* to assume that the dowager was a wanton, one who freely bestowed her favors upon him. Up until last autumn, it had suited their purpose to be regarded in such a light, being the perfect cover for the real purpose of their liaison—espionage against Napoleon's France.

His reverie was broken when the entrance of the Fairfax gatehouse loomed around the bend in the road. He urged Achilles forward, eager to end the journey. On reaching the stables, he handed the horse over to a groom and entered the house via the servant's entrance.

To his surprise, he found his mother, Mary, waiting for him at the top of the stairs.

"Oh dear," she said, turning her cheek for a filial kiss. "My heart sank when your man Hillman arrived with your luggage earlier on. I *prayed* that that black beast of yours would throw a shoe or something, forcing you to spend the night at an inn. But I suppose that was too much to ask for."

"I love you, too, Mother."

She looked contrite. "I do not mean to be unkind, darling, but we have guests this weekend and your father and I can certainly do without a repeat of all the trouble you caused the last visit you paid us."

"Mother, you are being unfair. That little to-do last month was none of my doing. But if you wish it, I shall proceed to Camberly and see you at your grandson's christening next Sunday."

Lady Fairfax patted his cheek. "That will not be necessary, darling. I would not dream of turning you away, but please be fair. One cannot consider the matter of Lord Edgerton breaking into your chamber in the middle of the night and finding his wife in your bed a little to-do."

"Her husband followed her there. I was sound asleep at the time and had no idea what was going on until that fool, Edgerton, grabbed me by the throat God knows I tried to talk him out of the duel."

"Your father and I are fully aware of the circumstances, Marcus, but could you try not to be *quite* so charming in the future? We are fast losing all of our friends, especially the ones with pretty wives."

"Heaven knows I make it a point not to dally with other men's wives. In the first place, I consider it to be bad form, and in the second place, I am not attracted to females who assume the role of predator. There is no challenge to it. It would be like a fox meekly surrendering to the hounds. If such were the case, it would not be worth the bother of getting out of bed to attend a hunt, now would it?"

Lady Fairfax frowned. "Oh, dear. What am I to do with you? Confusing fox hunts with affairs of the heart. The general idea is to get a bride *into* bed, not out of it. You will never be married the way you are going about it."

Marcus gave her a look. "Stop teasing. I fail to see the humor in the situation. I am sick of the constant hounding, especially by young things in their first Season. I had to boot young Caroline Ambrose out of my carriage last evening."

His mother kissed his cheek. "My poor darling. If you were

to take a bride, you would cut your troubles in half."

"You think so?"

"But of course, you silly boy. Granted, you are handsome, but to a husband-hunter, your main attraction is the earldom you will inherit and the riches that go with it. Only the widows and married ladies are interested in bedding you."

"Really, Mother, what a thing to say. I have no intention of getting married just to ward off an army of would-be wives."

His mother shrugged. "Then it would behoove you to stop complaining and start running a little faster, for sooner or later, one of those scheming little girls is bound to tree you."

Chapter 2

The following morning, Marcus rose at least two hours before his parents or any of their guests were likely to stir from their bed and ate breakfast amid the hustle and bustle of servants preparing for a new day. He then joined Hillman and Grimes at the stables to continue the journey to his brother John's house on the Sussex coast.

It was a cold morning, a light drizzle compounding the unpleasantness. On occasions that Marcus had been caught riding a horse in the rain, the three-caped coat he favored in cold weather had become a freezing, sodden weight. Not wishing to repeat the experience, he tied his mount, Achilles, to the side of the carriage and joined his valet inside.

Presently, weather cleared, but they encountered several more showers along the way. So upon reaching Camberly, Marcus was gratified to find the village was bathed in sunlight.

As the carriage turned into the entrance to Seaview House, he saw that his brother John, his wife, Althea, and sundry footmen were waiting in front of the massive doorway to greet him. One of the footmen had no sooner opened his carriage door than John waved him aside and gave Marcus a hand out of the conveyance.

"I am glad you have finally arrived. Althea has been driving me mad, conjecturing as to your arrival. She is dying for you to see how much your nephew has grown since your last visit."

"Been using her spyglass, I presume? She could not possibly have seen the carriage approach from around that curve in the road."

"You have the right of it, Marcus. Althea has had it trained on you for the last three miles of your journey."

"Has she, now?"

Marcus took the granite steps leading to the portal two at a time and gave his sister-in-law a brotherly hug, then held her away from him. "Althea, you look positively blooming. Motherhood suits you." He gave her cheek a playful pinch. "Or could it be that being married to my brother has put the roses in your cheeks?"

Althea broke free of his grasp and wagged her finger at him. "Marcus, you will cease the coy remarks this instant or I shall personally escort you back to your carriage." She softened the rebuke with a smile. "And the answer to your impertinent question is yes on both points. I love being Percy's mother"— she put her arm around John's waist—"almost as much as I love being married to his father."

Marcus gave John an arch smile. "I think it is safe to presume that being an ideal husband presents no problem for you."

John returned the smile. "I do not consider myself to be an ideal anything, but if I make a tolerable husband, I have Father's example to thank for it. He is an exemplary husband and father. None among our circle of friends had a happier childhood than we."

Marcus nodded. "I quite agree."

Althea gave John's waist a squeeze. "Your dear papa has my eternal gratitude, but let us not stay on these steps all afternoon extolling his virtues. A perfectly delicious luncheon has been prepared for us."

After eating, they withdrew to the library. John considered it the most comfortable room in the house. It certainly was his favorite, and unless they entertained guests, their reception rooms were seldom used.

Marcus strode over to the tall window facing the ocean. Althea's spyglass was on a nearby table. He picked it up and, placing it to his eye, made a sweeping survey of the bay.

"My goodness, if it were not for the trees I swear one would see all the way to Brighton. Hold on, I do believe Fennimore has the *Seafoam* moored in Camberly Bay directly south of the pier." He turned to the others. "Come and see for yourselves. I wonder what possible reason he could have to pull into Camberly now that Althea and her mama no longer intrigue with that seedy-looking spy. What was his name? Soapes? He certainly would have been the better for a bath or two."

John joined Marcus at the window and gave him a withering look. "I was called Soames, as well you know, since you came up with the name. A supposed smuggler can hardly haunt the seaports of England and France dressed like a crony of that Brummell fellow—and live to tell the tale."

Althea hastened to John's side and put a protective arm around his waist "Marcus, behave. John Soames might have been a little shabby around the edges, but he always looked clean." She rose on the tips of her toes and kissed her husband on the cheek. "I was sorely tempted to accept his offer of marriage."

Marcus raised a brow. "Really? A high-in-the-instep countess such as Althea Markham? I find that most shocking. What made you decide against the match?"

Althea shot John a rueful glance. "Forgive me, darling, but when we chanced to encounter one another on the village esplanade that afternoon, you were looking particularly dreadful."

John grinned. "I am not surprised you spurned my offer. Ever since your previous rejection of me, I had been drowning my sorrows in that excellent cognac I was given to smuggling and consequently had paid scant attention to my appearance."

Althea shook her head. "That is putting it mildly. Even so, I was enamored of you, and if you had not made the mistake of suggesting that I forsake my family at Camberly Hall to live under the roof that you would provide for me, I might have agreed to the union."

She wrinkled her nose. "You had torn the sleeve of that shabby jacket you favored, and it occurred to me that you might want to install me in one of those dreadful little hovels the fishermen live in just beyond the esplanade."

She gestured around the room. "How was I to know that you were the younger brother Marcus mentioned from time to time who had inherited this wonderful house from his aunt?"

"That is it? You chose John Ridley over John Soames

because you thought he owned the better house?" John looked reproachful. "You mercenary little baggage. And I thought you married me for my irresistible charm."

Marcus put a hand on John's shoulder. "If I were you, brother dear, I would end this conversation here and now. Camberly Hall, in all its magnificence, can be clearly seen across the bay. Granted, Seaview House is a handsome edifice but it can hardly compare with the palatial splendor of the countryseat of the Markhams'. Althea must truly love you to relinquish the keys of Camberly Hall to her mother for your sake."

John and Althea exchanged adoring looks. Marcus felt bereft. It must be heaven to love and be loved so profoundly, he thought. Then, with a shrug, he said, "We digress. As I recall, we were questioning Captain Fennimore's reason for bringing the *Seafoam* to Camberly Bay."

"Not *we. You*," John replied.

"Hmm?"

"*You* were doing the questioning. Althea and I are fairly sure what he is about. His being here has nothing to do with his duty to king and country and everything to do with the charms of the wanton little serving wench who works at the village tavern."

Marcus was surprised. "Betsy of the Boar's Head? Good heavens, is the man still making a fool of himself over that overheated little pea-goose?"

"I am afraid so," Althea added, pursing her lips. "I fear the girl makes him quite forget that he has a wife and five children living in Bournemouth." Althea gave John an aggrieved look. "Had I known that Captain Fennimore was so lacking in moral fiber I should not have consented to his marrying us that night on the *Seafoam.*"

Marcus could not resist the opportunity to tease her. "I must admit, sister-in-law, that it would have been better for me had you waited to be properly churched. When I knocked on the door to Camberly Hall that night and informed your mother that you had eloped with my brother on the *Seafoam* and not to expect you for breakfast on the morrow, I thought she would rip out my throat. As it was, her attitude toward me was decidedly cool for several weeks. For some reason, she laid the blame for your impetuous behavior at my door."

"As well she should," John replied. "The lady knows I lack the imagination to come up with such a scheme."

"All the same, her attitude cut me to the quick. I consider Celeste to be one of my dearest friends."

"You are most fortunate that my dear mother-in-law has a forgiving nature. She was feverishly making plans for us to renew our vows at St. Martin's when it became evident that Althea was with child."

"Exactly nine months and however long it took Fennimore to drop you ashore at Seaview," Marcus inserted slyly.

Althea colored. "I would be much obliged if you would put an end to this scandalous conversation, sirrah."

"Sirrah, is it?" Marcus affected an air of wounded sensibility. "I mean no harm, Althea. Truth be told, I envy the happiness that both of you share. If I could find a young lady who could love me as utterly and as sincerely as you love John, one I could love as deeply as he loves you, I would marry her in an instant."

John sighed. "Alas, brother, then you must resign yourself to a life of loneliness. I defy you to find any female among the *ton* who can hold a candle to my Althea." He stressed the point by bestowing a kiss upon his wife's generously curved lips.

His brother's words echoed like a death knell in Marcus's head. He gazed thoughtfully at his petite, fair-haired, green-eyed sister-in-law. She was both lovely and loving, not the sort of female who would stir his blood, thank heavens, but perfect in every way for his brother. But perhaps John had the right of it; God had not seen fit to create the perfect mate for him.

Marcus smiled. "I wish you could convince our mother of that. Then perhaps she would cease throwing every Bath miss she encounters at my feet."

He turned to Althea. "When will I be allowed to see my nephew? According to your mother, whom I met but two evenings ago, I understand you are harboring a de Maligny in your midst, with hair as fiery and as curly as her own."

Althea sighed. "I am afraid so. I just pray he has not inherited her predilection for getting into all sorts of mischief. Now if you will accompany me to the nursery, he should have finished his nap and be ready to give you one of his dazzling smiles. Something else he inherited from his grandmama, I might add."

On visiting the brightly painted, sunlit nursery, he regarded the pink-cheeked, rosy-lipped little cherub with the red-gold curls with awe. It did not seem possible that a scant six weeks prior, his nephew had been merely a subject for conjecture.

Would it be a boy or a girl? Would it take after John and have light brown hair? Or would it be blessed with Althea's luxuriant honey-blond curls? He had not even considered that the child would favor his grandmother Celeste.

Red hair, he decided, was absolutely perfect. He could not imagine how the baby could possibly have any other color and still be Percy. Marcus leaned over the crib and touched his tiny fingers. The little one immediately grasped his thumb and would not let go. Helpless to resist, Marcus surrendered his heart to the future Earl of Camberly.

Althea smiled at Marcus across the crib. "You have fallen under Percy's spell, I can tell."

"Am I that transparent?"

"Absolutely," Althea replied. "You look as I imagine Sir Galahad must have looked when he first beheld the Holy Grail."

"You have to admit that there is something both holy and miraculous about all new babies and Percy in particular," Marcus parried, feeling extremely uncomfortable at having exposed his feelings.

"We like to think so," John inserted. He exchanged smiles with Althea. "But we are probably no judges. We would think that of our son if he had entered the world in possession of two noses or twelve toes."

Althea lifted Percy from the crib and held him out to Marcus. "Would you like to hold him?"

Marcus took a step back. "Do you think it wise? I know nothing about infants."

Althea gave him an encouraging smile. "You will learn. Babies do not come with instructions. Just coo at him and do your best not to drop him, and I am sure you will both get along splendidly."

Marcus cradled the baby in the crook of his arm. Percy regarded him with deep blue eyes and smiled. Marcus felt his bones turn to butter.

He looked up and caught Althea and John exchanging delighted grins. He immediately handed Percy back to Althea. "Here. It will not work. Neither one of you is subtle enough to pull it off."

John affected an air of complete bafflement, but Marcus was not deceived. "Percy is a charmer, and you are right, Althea, he does get it from Celeste, but if you think that my melting all over your son and heir is going to inspire me to dash out and marry the first Bath miss who happens to cross my path in order to father a Percy of my own, you are sadly mistaken."

Althea gave him a look that implied he was foaming at the mouth. "What an odd thing to say." She looked to John. "Most odd, do you not agree, darling?"

"Absolutely. Most odd," John rejoined.

Althea directed a sweet smile at Marcus. Marcus was not deceived. He braced himself for what was undoubtedly to follow.

Althea nodded. "Beyond odd, actually. Marcus held our son in his arms for less than a minute and began to babble about brides and babies with that fevered look in his eye. How else would one describe such behavior?"

Althea and John exchanged knowing smiles over the top of Percy's curly head. Marcus was not amused.

"You have had your fun. Now do me the kindness of wiping those silly grins off your faces. I will give you this much: the thought of having a son like Percy does hold an attraction, but toward such an end, I would not marry where my heart does not lie."

John looked contrite. "Of course you would not. It was clumsy of us. Althea and I just thought a little nudge in the right direction would push you into a more sincere effort in seeking a bride. You must admit, Marcus, that you have not given a moment's consideration to any of the young ladies who have shown an interest in you."

"Nor will I. When the right girl for me puts in an appearance, she will not have to give me a second glance, *I* shall recognize *her* in an instant and happily pursue her to the ends of the earth, if need be. In the meantime…"

Marcus did not continue, deeming that telling his well-meaning brother and sister-in-law to mind their own business was not quite the thing. He only hoped that when his parents arrived for Percy's christening on the weekend they would not join forces with John and Althea to hammer home the joys of marital bliss.

Clarissa Carter carried a small basket of apples into the kitchen and handed them over to Mrs. Gates, the family cook.

The plump, motherly looking servant rooted through the wizened fruit and sniffed. "Poor looking things, I must say."

"It cannot be helped. After all, they have been in the storage cellar since last autumn. Never mind," Clarissa soothed, "after they are sliced and soaked in water, they will make tolerable pies. Especially if *you* put them together. No one has your magic with pastry, Mrs. Gates."

Mrs. Gates' ample bosom visibly swelled. "It is very good of you to say so, Miss Clarissa, especially since you have partaken of the pies that come out of his lordship's kitchens."

"The pies at the Towers might look very grand, but for all their fancy pastry work, when it comes to pleasing the palate, they do not hold a candle to yours."

Mrs. Gates patted Clarissa on the cheek. This required much stretching on her part, for at an inch short of six feet, Clarissa towered over her.

Mrs. Gates bustled over to the larder and returned with a plate of sugar biscuits and a mug of milk. "Here, my lamb, get these down you. I am afraid if you get any thinner, you are going to blow away on the next good breeze we get."

Clarissa twirled a tendril of bright red hair that had escaped from the confines of a bandeau. "Mama says that as soon as I have finished my growth spurt, I should fill out nicely."

"Good heavens, child, it is to be hoped you will not grow any taller. As it is, you tower over all the lads who are likely to come a courting. The only one in this parish who is taller than you is his lordship's son and heir, and he is not likely to come to *this* house to seek a bride."

Clarissa felt her throat constrict Surely Mrs. Gates did not suspect the *tendre* she carried in her heart for Marcus Ridley?

She affected an air of nonchalance. "I should hope *not*. Lord Ridley is *far too* full of himself for my liking."

Mrs. Gates looked skeptical. "Really, now? Is that why you chased after him all over the Fairfax estate when you were a child? Fair hounded him to death. I cannot for the life of me understand how he put up with you."

"You are mistaken, Mrs. Gates. It was his brother John whom I liked, and then only as a friend. My goodness, I was very young then."

Mrs. Gates smiled. "Of course you were. Speaking of our betters, Mr. Gates happened to mention that Lord and Lady Fairfax returned from their grandson's christening yesterday afternoon, and it seems that Lord Ridley accompanied them on the journey."

"Indeed?" Clarissa replied, hoping she had injected the proper degree of disinterest ino her tone.

Mrs. Gates nodded. "I understand that he is not continuing his journey to London until the morrow."

Clarissa gulped down her milk. "I think I shall take a little stroll down the lane to walk off those biscuits."

"I think that is most wise," Mrs. Gates replied. "By all means get out while the sun is shining. One never knows how long the good weather is going to last in April. I believe it was that heavy downpour we suffered yesterday that convinced Lord Ridley to stay over for a day or two. Give the roads a chance to dry out."

As soon as Clarissa was out of view of any onlookers, she raised her skirts and hared down the lane until she came to a stile affording access to a meadow abutting the stately gardens of Fairfax Towers. Raising her skirts even higher, she threaded her way around a herd of cud-chewing bovines, taking care to avoid what the Ridley boys had taught her to refer to as "cow pies."

On reaching the edge of a large stretch of lawn, Clarissa stopped at the foot of an ancient oak tree. Its gnarled trunk had enormous girth, with enough nodes and hollows to offer footholds sufficient to reach the branches, which soared out and up with awe-inspiring majesty.

Clarissa grabbed an overhanging bough and attempted to put her foot in a hollow, but the skirt of her white muslin dress got in her way. "Botheration," she muttered, and tucked the hem into the blue sash girding the high waistline.

She then climbed the tree with a speed and skill that bespoke many years of practice in the doing. Several sparrows flew from the branches, twittering in outrage at the intrusion.

On reaching a sturdy branch that afforded her a clear view of Fairfax Towers, she pulled down her skirt in a vain effort to cover her pantalettes. Giving up on the attempt, she settled down on a branch and pressed her back firmly against the broad tree trunk.

"Perfect," she murmured. "When Marcus takes the air after luncheon; I shall have a perfect view. It will be like the old days—almost." Then she sighed, knowing that nothing could ever be quite the same.

In the old days, Marcus and John had let her tag along after them. Marcus had taught her how to climb trees, starting with the oak she now straddled in such an unladylike fashion.

When Lord and Lady Fairfax entertained guests on the lawns in the summer and she knew Marcus was there, from the vantage point of the old oak, Clarissa never failed to watch the festivities. It was her only tie to the happy time when she was too young to be considered an unsuitable companion for the sons of the Earl of Fairfax.

Clarissa's idyll ended abruptly the year that Marcus was enrolled in Eton. The following year, John joined him and later followed him to Oxford.

It was when John went up to Oxford that Clarissa was sent, at her mother's insistence, to live with her father's older brother in Derbyshire.

Uncle Henry had not only inherited the family's modest fortune, through shrewd investments in the tea and spice trades he had made it grow to a tidy sum, thereby affording his three daughters the advantage of a fine house and an excellent governess—advantages of which Clarissa was sorely in need, according to her mother.

Clarissa was returned to the bosom of her family the previous August, four months before her seventeenth birthday. Her mother could see little improvement in Clarissa's deportment and did little to hide her dismay.

A week after returning to Fairfax, Clarissa had had difficulty sleeping and had overheard her mother exclaim, "But, Thomas, she is so *tall*. Why, oh, why, does she have to take after you? And those freckles on her nose! I blame Alice for that. You may be sure that *her* daughters were protected from the sun."

"Now, now, Beatrice, be fair. I defy anyone to convince Clarissa to conduct herself otherwise. She has not an ounce of vanity."

As Clarissa wriggled into a more comfortable position on the tree branch, she recalled her mother's scathing criticism and her father's response to it.

At the time, she had resented his words. Now, looking at the mud smearing her dress, she had to admit that perhaps her father's assessment of her character was correct Clarissa shrugged, deciding there were mitigating circumstances.

I am tall and ungainly, and nothing can change that. Besides, I have grown at least another inch since Mama lodged her complaint. She gave a little giggle. *Vanity, on my part, of necessity, would be in vain.*

Clarissa's feeble attempt at humor was doomed to be short-lived, for at that very moment a huge drop of rain landed squarely on the tip of her nose, to be followed by more drops, seemingly larger and gaining in frequency.

At the onset of the shower, she toyed with the idea of climbing back down the tree to retrace her steps across the meadow, but decided against it. After all, from past experience, she knew that the oak leaves should afford her some measure of protection against the rain.

It did not take her long to regret this decision. All too soon she became thoroughly soaked and felt absolutely miserable. Then it occurred to her that so early in the year, the tree had yet to come into full leaf and had very little shelter to offer from the downpour.

This led her to a more dire realization. If the tree lacked sufficient foliage to protect her from the rain, it certainly would not have enough to screen her from the view of a passerby.

As these thoughts occurred to her, the shower stopped just as abruptly as it started. She attempted the descent down the tree branches, but found her hands were too numb with cold to grasp the tree limbs as firmly as safety required.

She resumed her position against the tree trunk and vigorously rubbed her hands together until she felt the life return to her fingertips. The pain of the blood coursing through her fingers once more brought tears to her eyes.

"Botheration!" she exclaimed. "Why do I subject my person to such indignities? I would be far better off helping Mrs. Gates peel apples in front of a cozy fire."

Why bother with this self-delusion? I would brave far worse for but a glimpse of Marcus.

Clarissa suddenly grasped a branch and edged her way to a lower footing. "Anything, that is, but the risk of being caught by Marcus in such humiliating circumstances. Oh Lord, let me come through this without getting caught, and I promise to mend my ways."

Her outburst was followed by a wail of despair, for in the distance, she espied the object of her abject devotion resolutely striding in her direction.

In an act of sheer desperation, she scrambled up to the higher branches of the oak, in the forlorn hope that Marcus might keep his eyes focused on where he was putting his feet and not notice her presence.

Unfortunately, Marcus came ever nearer, his head held high and whistling a cheerful tune.

Chapter 3

As soon as the rain stopped, Marcus hurried outside intending to walk off the heavy luncheon in which he had indulged. He was beginning to regret his decision to stay the extra two days at Fairfax Towers. In his opinion, far too much food was served at his father's table and, unfortunately, all of it was delicious and hard to resist

"Why on earth did I let Mother talk me into staying over? If I had not been so damned bored, I would not have made such a pig of myself," he muttered. "What is worse, whatever made me suggest at Percy's christening that she trot out some suitable girls for me to meet? I must have been absolutely round the bend."

Deciding to lay the subject to rest, he started to whistle a doubtful little ditty left over from his Oxford days. He had traversed but a third of the way across the lawn when he caught a flash of white among the foliage of the old oak tree. He stopped whistling and narrowed his eyes to afford a better view. It looked like a covey of white doves, but he deemed this unlikely.

Then he caught sight of a human face peering through the leaves. A female in a white muslin dress, scrambling high among the branches of the huge oak? That was absurd. Besides, the only female he knew who came close to being that tall was his mother, and climbing a tree would be the last thing on earth that would occur to her.

Marcus quickened his pace, determined to solve the mystery as soon as possible. To his surprise, the glimpses of white were on the ascent and fast reaching branches that were far too flimsy to hold weight of any consequence.

Marcus broke into a run and did not stop until he had

reached the oak tree. From amid the branches he saw the pinched white face of a young girl, framed by a mop of dripping wet red curls.

"What do you think you are doing, young lady?"

The girl opened her mouth as if in response, but apparently thought better of it, and clamped it shut.

"No matter," he added. "Come down as fast as you can. That branch is not strong enough to hold your weight I'll climb up and speed things along."

Before Marcus could make good on his promise, there was an ominous cracking of wood, followed by an ear-piercing shriek. Amid a shower of splintered wood and wet leaves, the girl landed on top of him, the brunt of her weight targeting his breadbasket.

"Oof!" With the breath knocked out of him, Marcus just lay there, unable to do anything about the girl, who lay sprawled over him. It occurred to him that she was the first Bath miss with whom he had experienced such intimate contact, and he found it not in the least pleasant In fact he feared he was in danger of losing the luncheon he had all too recently wolfed down.

Before it came to this, the girl rolled over and sprang to her feet. From where he lay, her long, lean body seemed to stretch to infinity, the fiery nimbus encircling her hair rendering her appearance strange, otherworldly.

This feeling was dispelled when, with a determined grimace, she grasped him firmly by the hand and elbow and pulled him to his feet.

"I say, I am dreadfully sorry about that," she exclaimed, her forehead knitted in concern. "I hope I did not inflict any serious harm upon your person."

Marcus felt angry and out of sorts over the situation and was tempted to give her a thorough set-down. But that was before her eyes filled with what seemed to be genuine concern.

Instead his anger turned to pity. He doubted she would ever be pretty. She was far too thin. Her face was pinched looking and lacking in feminine appeal, he thought.

He gave her a second look. The freckles and the dreadful

bird's nest of bright red curls notwithstanding, she did have a pair of fine eyes of a most extraordinary shade. Not quite blue and certainly not green. Aquamarine. That was it. Aquamarine.

Unfortunately, her eyes, however beautiful, would not compensate for the hollow face in which they were set. Few men could match her in height, and he recalled having encountered scarecrows that filled out their clothes to better advantage.

"I am quite all right, thank you," he responded. "I trust you have sustained no injury?"

She looked rueful. "A few scratches and, no doubt some dreadful bruises. A tree branch took the brunt of my fall. Otherwise I shudder to think what injuries you might have sustained."

"Hmmm, quite. I suggest that in the future, you refrain from climbing trees. It is hardly the thing for a female to do, would you not agree?"

She shrugged. "If you are of that opinion, my lord, why did you teach me how in the first place?"

Marcus inhaled. "Taught you *how?* What nonsense is this?"

The girl smiled. Marcus was fascinated by the transformation. Every moveable feature on her face crinkled upward.

She looks impish. I feel as if I know her, but dashed if I can place her.

He searched her face. "Clarissa? Clarissa Carter? I never would have recognized you. You were such a plump little girl, chasing after my brother and me like—"

"An annoying little gnat? I am afraid the gnat has turned into one of those nasty looking spiders. What are they called? Ah yes, daddy longlegs."

Marcus was about to offer a little white lie, likening her to a colt rather than a spider. Then he realized by the mischievous grin on her face that she was not in the least bit perturbed over the matter.

"Might I ask what on earth you were doing in the oak tree in the middle of a rain shower? And here, to boot? As I recall, there are sufficient trees in the Carter garden to satisfy such an urge."

"Yes, but all kinds of interesting things take place over here.

Nothing exciting *ever* happens in our garden."

Marcus was aghast. "Do you mean to stand there and tell me that you come over here for the sole purpose of spying on my family? How could you? It is outside of outrageous."

"I am sorry, Marcus. I did not see my actions in that light. The oak was the first tree you taught me to climb and it is special to me."

"For heaven's sake, Clarissa, surely you have better things to do? Have you no friends?"

Clarissa shrugged. "Whom would you suggest? The young milkmaids who work in your dairy? Or the ones who scrub the floors and vats in your cheesery? They would reject my company just as swiftly as would the daughters of the local gentry."

Marcus shook his head. "I was not suggesting that you mingle with the farm people. For the most part, the villagers are good, decent folk, but are illiterate. You would have nothing in common. But take Squire Cobbett's twins, Lavinia and Leticia. I am sure they would welcome your friendship. Perhaps my mother can arrange something."

Clarissa pulled away from his grasp. "Please, I beg of you. I should be mortified. I am not at all the sort of person that the Cobbett twins could warm to. I have no small talk and cannot generate the sort of enthusiasm for clothes and fripperies that they demand in a friend."

"Then involving Lady Fairfax would be a complete waste of time." He tried to look as stern as possible. "That notwithstanding, you cannot continue this folly of climbing other people's trees."

Clarissa's lower lip quivered. He decided on a softer approach.

"After all, Clarissa, my dear, you must realize that you have reached an age that renders such a practice most improper. Promise me that I shall not catch you doing it again."

Clarissa gave him a tremulous smile. "I promise."

Marcus beamed at her. "That's the thing. Now come with me. I cannot allow you to go home in that state. You would catch your death of cold."

"B-but—"

"No 'buts,' young lady. Your teeth are beginning to chatter. I am sure my mother can find you something to wear while your own things dry."

Marcus decided that his best course of action was to deposit Clarissa below stairs in the capable hands of Mrs. Cole, the housekeeper, before involving his mother in the situation. With this thought in mind, he ushered Clarissa through the kitchen garden and into Fairfax Towers via the servant's entrance.

As fate would have it, they encountered Mrs. Cole in the long flagstone hallway leading to the kitchen. The housekeeper was one of those English women with skin as thin as paper and crazed like poorly fired porcelain. She listened to Marcus's edited version of what had befallen Clarissa, her upper lip pursed into deep grooves of disapproval.

At the conclusion of his story as to how Miss Carter had been caught in the rain while strolling in the meadow, Mrs. Cole accorded the shivering girl a pinch-nosed sniff.

"Young lady, I cannot imagine what you were thinking, haring about the country at this time of year without as much as a shawl to cover your shoulders. Mark my words, you will be lucky to escape the lung fever."

"To that end, I think a bath should be drawn for Miss Carter and sent up to one of the guest chambers. In the meantime, I shall prevail upon Lady Fairfax to provide something of hers for the young lady to wear while her own garments are drying."

Mrs. Cole's eyebrows flew up into inverted vees. "Prevail upon your lady mother to provide this feckless creature with something to wear from her own clothespress? Really, Lord Ridley, that is most untoward, and I am sure her ladyship will be quick to tell you so."

Marcus laughed. "Nonsense, Mrs. Cole, her ladyship will not mind in the least She lacks your predilection for snobbery."

Mrs. Cole's bosom puffed up. "Well, I never. How could you call me a snob, sir? I am only the housekeeper."

Marcus was only too happy to enlighten her. "Mrs. Cole, are you not a stickler for keeping others in their proper place?"

She looked shocked. "But of course, sir. Things run much more smoothly that way. I do not belong in the withdrawing room taking refreshments with her ladyship and her friends, no more than she belongs in the kitchen interfering with the way cook prepares a pork pie for your luncheon. Surely you can see that, sir?"

"Absolutely, Mrs. Cole, but your being right does not absolve you from the snobbery such a position calls for. In the meantime, if it will make you feel any better, rest assured that the daughter of our Mr. Carter is a perfectly respectable young lady and the roof will not fall about your ears if you treat her as such."

Mrs. Cole's faded blue eyes widened in surprise. "This is *our* Mr. Carter's Clarissa?"

Clarissa raised her chin. "Yes, I am."

"I always thought you took after your mother, what with you being such a small child and having her ginger hair an' all. And here you are, as tall as her ladyship, I shouldn't wonder."

Mrs. Cole took a step back and with a finger on her chin put Clarissa to close scrutiny. "Hmmm, yes. Now that you have grown up, I can see that you look more like your father."

Clarissa grimaced. "So I am told."

Marcus searched her face for any signs of distress at the housekeeper's words and was relieved to see that Clarissa seemed quite at ease. Such a hurt would be far more difficult to take care of than the scraped knees of her childhood. Then, a little lighthearted banter and the promise of a treat from the kitchen had been enough to chase away her tears.

"I am sorry, Clarissa," Mrs. Cole continued. "I mistook you for one of those foolish females who are constantly trying to trick poor Lord Ridley into marriage. I should have realized that such was not the case."

Clarissa gave a dry laugh. "Since I am not in possession of a magic wand, such an attempt on my part could offer little hope for success. Besides, what chance for happiness could there be in an arrangement whereby a gentleman is tricked into a marriage not of his choosing?"

Marcus responded with a laugh that bordered on the sardonic. "I rather suspect that for such creatures, the hope of one day becoming the Countess of Fairfax would be happiness enough."

Clarissa turned to Marcus, her eyes filled with concern. "Oh, dear. Surely one or two of these young ladies must truly care for you, my lord? You might be a trifle high-handed at times, but you have a kind heart, and I understand that most females consider you to be quite handsome."

Marcus was taken aback. *One* or *two* must truly care for him? *Most* females were said to consider him to be quite handsome? *Quite handsome?* Faint praise indeed from a quintessential wallflower.

Suddenly Marcus recognized his piqued vanity for what it was and gave a deprecating shrug. "I suppose the odd one liked me well enough, but that is neither here nor there."

"It is not?"

"Of course not. I have yet to find a young lady whose company I can tolerate for a week, much less a lifetime."

Marcus paused to take a breath, and Mrs. Cole filled the lull in the conversation with a contrived cough. Marcus pulled up short. What on earth had possessed him to touch on such a personal topic as love and matrimony with the steward's daughter—and in front of Mrs. Cole, of all people?

Truth be told, he had completely forgotten the housekeeper's presence. But even so, what was it about Clarissa Carter that had inspired him to babble on about things that were none of her concern?

Perhaps the bond they had formed in childhood? After all, he had taught her to climb to heights at which many a boy would have balked. Then he dismissed this notion out of hand. There had been no bond between them. She had merely been an annoying little insect who had refused to be shooed away.

Then he realized it was because he felt comfortable with Clarissa Carter. Not once had she flirted with him either with word or gesture. Indeed, she had attempted not so much as the bat of an eye, and that was why he did not feel the need for the defensive stance he usually adopted when in the company of marriageable females.

Pushing such thoughts aside, he addressed the housekeeper. "Mrs. Cole, I shall leave Miss Carter in your capable hands while I see Lady Fairfax about finding her something suitable to wear."

Mrs. Cole responded with a slight bob. "Very good, sir. I have a nice fire going in my room with a kettle boiling on the hob. I think Miss Carter would feel better if she had a nice cup of tea. I know I would."

Marcus nodded in approval and made his way up the stairs to the main hall where he encountered Sanders, the butler.

"Good afternoon, my lord. I trust you enjoyed your walk. The gardens always seem more fragrant after a shower."

"Oh, quite," Marcus rejoined. "By the way, I should like someone to inform the Carters that their daughter, Clarissa, sought refuge from the storm here and not to worry. She will be delivered to them safe and sound in an hour or so."

Clarissa arrived home two hours later and entered their modest parlor to find her mother turning from the window, a look of discontent marring her handsome face.

"I see that one of the grooms brought you home in the old wagon used for running errands."

"And I was grateful for her ladyship's kindness. I did not relish getting my feet wet after the rain."

"But the old *wagon*? It is so demeaning. What if the Cobbett twins had happened by?"

"Come now, Mama. Surely you did not expect me to be returned in the family carriage?"

Mrs. Carter clutched at a locket nestled among the folds of a silk fichu adorning the neckline of her dress, bringing to Clarissa's attention that her mother was wearing her best afternoon dress of a russet twilled silk and the cap of fine Nottingham lace she wore only for special occasions.

"Try not to be so foolish, Clarissa," she replied. "Of course you would not have been given the brougham. But I rather expected the viscount to escort you home in some sort of conveyance that a friendship of long-standing such as yours would warrant."

"A friendship such as ours? Mama, it was he who dubbed me Gnat. That scarcely denotes a friendship of any sort."

"Nonsense. I am sure it denotes a certain fondness."

A rustling noise made Clarissa aware that her father was seated in his favorite armchair by the hearth, a newspaper in his hands. He looked askance at his wife, rolled his eyes, and, as was his wont, promptly returned to reading the latest news to come out of London.

Clarissa sighed. "Marcus Ridley called me Gnat because I was a pest. At no time did he show by word or deed that he considered me to be a friend."

"But—"

"For pity's sake, Beatrice, let the matter drop. If Clarissa says that no friendship exists between them, have the good sense to believe her," Edwin Carter rejoined. "Not that I'm surprised. I warned you that no good could come of letting the child roam all over the countryside chasing after those two boys. How they put up with her, I'll never know."

"But something *could* have come of it." Mrs. Carter said plaintively. "Of course, I realized that an alliance with the older boy was unlikely. Apart from his superior good looks, his being heir to the earldom put him far from Clarissa's reach, but his brother, John, was another matter entirely."

Clarissa gave a dry laugh. "Your expectations for me were far too high. It is generally acknowledged that John Ridley made the most brilliant match for many a Season."

"And he being such an ordinary looking man."

"Those who do not know him very well might think so, Mama, but I believe he has a forthright spirit and a most engaging smile, virtues that evidently did not go unnoticed by the Countess of Camberly."

"Humph! It is most unfortunate that he did not find you equally engaging," her mother replied. "And to think of all the sacrifices I made to such an end."

"S-sacrifices, Mama? I do not understand."

"No. I do not suppose you do." Mrs. Carter held out the skirt to her dress. "Why do you suppose I still receive ladies of the village wearing this rag?"

"Rag? But is it not your best afternoon dress?"

"And is likely to be until it falls off my back in tatters. Every penny we could spare went to clothe you as befits a member of your Uncle Henry's household. Let me tell you, miss, your growing out of everything with such alarming regularity did not help matters."

"For pity's sake, Beatrice, let the subject drop," Mr. Carter remonstrated. "You talk as if Clarissa grew out of her clothes just to annoy you."

Mrs. Carter gave him a rueful smile. "Forgive me. I know Clarissa cannot be held to account for that. Only I had such high hopes for her." She sighed. "Clarissa was such an adorable little poppet. Who would have—"

Who would have, indeed? Clarissa thought. *One would think I enjoyed being such an oddity. Yes, oddity. That was the word the Cobbett twins used to describe me coming out of church last Sunday.*

"I am sure *some* good will come of rounding out our girl's education," Mr. Carter soothed. "There are one or two widowers in these parts with decent estates who might overlook the lack of dowry in a second wife. Especially a young one."

Clarissa felt her stomach lurch. "Papa, how could you suggest such a thing? I thought you loved me."

"I do, child. With all my heart. What sort of life should I wish for you, pray tell? Would you rather grow old as the companion of a spoiled, demanding old dowager? Or perhaps as a governess, taking care of another woman's children?"

"Either occupation would be far more honorable than marriage to a man I do not love."

"More honorable than marriage?" Mrs. Carter brushed the back of her hand across her forehead and sank onto a faded gold damask sofa. "Edwin, I think I am going to faint."

Mr. Carter put down his newspaper with an impatient snap. "Not now, Beatrice, I am in no mood for drama. If Clarissa wishes to become a governess, I certainly shall not stand in her way. Heaven knows, marriage is not always a bed of roses."

Mrs. Carter leaped to her feet her fit of the vapors forgotten. "Just what do you mean by that remark, Mr. Carter?" She dabbed her right eye with the back of her hand. "Have I not been an exemplary wife? Have I not made every sacrifice to see to your comfort? Have I—"

"Say no more, my dear. It is as you say. I was referring to marriage in general, not our little haven of wedded bliss. Ours was a love match, was it not?"

Mrs. Carter clutched her bosom and rewarded her spouse with a tremulous smile. "I am relieved to hear you say so. My every thought is for your happiness."

Thankful that her mother did not catch the irony in her father's tone, and even more thankful that she was no longer the focus of her parents' attention, Clarissa thought it was the perfect time to make an escape. Alas, before she could reach the door, her mother barked an order for her to stay, in a voice carrying the full authority of a sergeant major.

"I do not remember dismissing you, young lady."

"I was just going to my chamber to put away my hat and gloves."

"What hat and gloves, pray? You run around like a common peasant at every possible chance, and it has to stop. I *will not* have you ruining your chances for a proper place in society."

"A proper place in society? Mama, please do not tease me. What place in society could I possibly hope for?"

"You must carve your own niche."

Mr. Carter rose from his chair. "What folly are you embarking upon this time, Beatrice? I think you do our daughter more harm than good with your fruitless little schemes."

His wife wheeled to face him. "I have no scheme. I merely wish our daughter to make full use of the opportunities that happen her way."

Clarissa saw a frown knit her father's brow and hoped her mother would tread softly. Mr. Carter was a reasonable man, but even he had his limits. To her relief, he sat down once more.

"Clarissa enjoys the friendship of Lord Ridley," Mrs.

Carter continued.

"I thought I explained—" Clarissa was discouraged from saying anything further by a dismissive wave from her mother.

"Call it what you like, Clarissa. He accords you his gracious condescension, as does his dear mother. She has always held you in kind regard. Probably because she lacks a daughter of her own."

"Balderdash!" her father inserted. "Then why did his lordship go to the trouble of giving our Thomas an education so that he could become a schoolmaster in a very prestigious boys' school? Lord and Lady Fairfax do not lack for sons. Pray do not read any more into their kindness than is intended."

His wife shrugged. "As you say, dear. I am merely pointing out that in enjoying the gracious condescension of her betters, our daughter is likely to be invited to some of the functions at Fairfax Towers. At least some of the lesser ones, and that would be to the good."

"I still do not see where this conversation is leading."

"It is simple. If she is invited to the less illustrious parties, she is liable to meet a young gentleman who is not quite so high in the instep. One who, though of good family, cannot possibly aspire to marrying a highborn lady. One whom Clarissa can find it in her heart to love."

Clarissa shook her head. "Mama, I fear your plans for me are doomed from the start."

Mrs. Carter threw up her hands. "You are not even willing to try. Go ahead. Become a governess or a lady's companion. Perhaps that is all you deserve."

"Look at me, Mama. Even if I had a dowry, which I do not, you would be hard put to find someone to take me off your hands. I am an oddity. Ask Leticia and Lavinia Cobbett. They will tell you so."

Mrs. Carter puffed up with indignation. "Those dreadful girls said that to your face? The cruel little cats."

"No, Mama, they did not say it to my face. Lavinia and Leticia are too well brought up not to observe all the proper hypocrisies of polite society."

"Proper hypocrisies? I declare, child, I sometimes wonder at the workings of your mind."

All of a sudden, the energy drained from Clarissa and she lost the desire to continue the exchange of words with her mother.

"If you please, Mama, I should like to go to my room. I am feeling very tired."

Mrs. Carter gave her a dismissive wave. "Run along, dear. I daresay a nap before dinner will do you good."

As Clarissa climbed the stairs, she heard her mother's voice waft out of the parlor. "We shall have to have an evening dress made for Clarissa. I will not have her in the position of having to have to turn down such an invitation for lack of the proper attire."

Then her father's gruff voice made answer. "Mrs. Carter, I declare that any spare coin I might have must needs go to house you in a suitable asylum, for of a certainty you have taken leave of your senses."

Chapter 4

Marcus slipped his arms into the dark gray evening coat Hillman held out for him, cursing the fact that it did not feel too comfortable around the armhole seams.

Hillman stepped back to admire the results. "Just as I thought, sir, the plum and silver waistcoat is sheer perfection with the gray."

"That is all very well, Hillman, but I think I would sell my soul if it would afford me a coat that fitted as well as it looks. I patronize the finest tailors that London has to offer, to no avail."

"I understand that it is even worse for the ladies, sir. For the most part, the fastenings to their garments are supplemented by the use of pins."

Marcus grimaced. "As well I know. One has to be careful not to sustain a prick to the hand while squiring some ladies around a ballroom floor. One would think that these clothiers would have perfected their craft by now. After all, mankind has availed themselves of their services almost from the time Adam and Eve were asked to vacate Eden."

"Harrumph! Quite, my lord."

A peal of girlish laughter emanating directly outside Marcus's chambers brought the conversation regarding the shortcomings of tailors and mantua makers to an abrupt end.

Marcus winced. "Heavens, what sort of a pickle has my mother put me in? When I consented to attend this weekend party, I *specifically* requested that no silly young girls in their first Season be included."

"I am sure her ladyship did her best. Some of the older maiden ladies are apt to be—um." Hillman halted, his brow furrowed as he searched for the appropriate words. "Antidotes,

I believe is the term I am looking for. Yes, that's it. Antidotes. Her ladyship merely wishes to spare you the ordeal of spending the weekend with ill-favored spinsters who have been gathering dust on the shelf, so to speak."

"I cannot agree," Marcus rejoined. "Many a comely girl has been consigned to the shelf because of all the good men who have died in this infernal war on the Peninsula."

"How very true."

"Dash it all, Hillman, I am not looking for a raving beauty. For one thing, I have found such creatures to be far too in love with themselves for my liking."

"Quite so," Hillman offered.

"All I am seeking is a fairly pleasant looking girl. One who makes one feel comfortable, definitely fun to be with. I could not abide a skittish creature who is afraid of her own shadow."

"Is that all, sir?"

Marcus suddenly felt sheepish. "Not quite, Hillman. She would have to be as madly, deeply in love with me as I with her."

Hillman looked thoughtful. "What you are saying, sir, is that you will consent only to a love match of legendary proportions?"

"A fanciful description, Hillman, but more or less correct."

"Oh dear. Then I fear her ladyship is wasting her time. I doubt such a love exists. After all, sir, legends are not called *such* without good reason."

Marcus raised both brows. "Good for you, Hillman. I had no idea you were such a perspicacious fellow."

Hillman inclined his head. "One does one's best sir."

The longcase clock in the entry hall on the floor below began to chime. Marcus grimaced. "Half past seven. Time to socialize with all the dewy-eyed young maidens and their parents my mother has invited for the weekend."

"My goodness, there is more than one of them, sir? Is that not a trifle awkward?"

"Awkward? No. The young ladies in question have no idea that they are being trotted out for inspection. But I rather expect it to be a dreadful bore."

Marcus took his leave of his valet and descended the grand

staircase leading to the entry hall. From here the voices of his parents' guests emanated from the large drawing room adjoining the dining room, a high, piping girlish voice making itself heard above the rest.

"What was my mother thinking?" he muttered. "Revenge—that's it. It has to be. Paying me back for that little run-in I had with Lord Edgerton. Most uncalled for, I must say. I went out of my way to do him but the merest of damage."

Upon entering the drawing room, Marcus was pounced upon at the door by his mother. "Marcus, you are late," she said, her voice scarcely above a whisper. "It really does not speak well of you."

"My apologies, Mother. The water for my bath was not heated in time."

"Never mind. Greet our guests. I wish you to accord special attention to a Miss Dianthus Gray when you are introduced. She is to be your dinner partner this evening."

"Dash it all, Mother, I have never met the girl. I see Eleanor Simpson has been invited. She is a good sort. I would far rather have her for a dinner partner." *Far rather. That bluestocking is not in the least bit interested in someone like me.*

"She *was* going to be, but while waiting for you she became engrossed in a conversation with Mr. Latham, you know, the young gentleman who is the expert on all things Greek. Eleanor made it known, quite nicely, of course, that rather than wait for you to put in an appearance she preferred to be seated next to Mr. Latham."

"And Sarah Haynes?" *Lady Sarah is far too proper to give a chap any trouble.*

His mother's face visibly brightened. "Really? She would be *my* choice, of course, but I only included her as a faint, far hope. Unfortunately, Miss Gray has already been informed of the arrangements, so you will just have to go along with them."

Before Marcus could respond, the girlish voice he had begun to dread trilled above the others once more. Marcus shuddered. *"Please* tell me that that nerve-shattering laugh does not belong to her."

"No, thank heavens. That would be her younger sister, Primrose. The older Miss Gray is far more circumspect."

Marcus gave a slight bow. "In which case, Mother, I hasten to do your bidding."

Marcus quickly made his way around the room, greeting those he knew and suffering introductions to those he did not. On being introduced to Dianthus Gray, he was relieved to discern that her voice was, indeed, low pitched and pleasant.

Although quite beautiful, her fair coloring was not to his taste. He preferred more vibrant looking women, the sort whose looks and manners bespoke, and usually delivered, nights filled with passion. Nevertheless, he decided that if only to please his mother, he would return to her side as soon as he was through with the social niceties.

This noble resolve was immediately forgotten by the disquietude he suffered upon seeing his good friend Bertram Thistlethwaite numbered among the guests. It had been a scant three months since Marcus had hosted a riotous farewell party in Town to celebrate Bertie's newly acquired captaincy and his subsequent departure to the warfront.

Anxious to learn what dire circumstances, if any, had brought Bertie back to England, Marcus rushed to his side, according those in his path the briefest of bows and how-do-you-dos.

Bertie was staring at the ceiling, seemingly oblivious to everyone else in the room. Marcus found this most disturbing. He had known Bertie since they had shared accommodations at Eton. "Cell mates," Bertie had dubbed them, and Marcus knew his friend was not given to introspection.

On reaching him, Marcus cleared his throat Bertie gave a start, grasped his hand, and pumped it vigorously, a beaming smile wreathing his face.

"Marcus, old chap. I was wondering when you would put in an appearance. You should be warned, your father was grumbling about your tardiness only a few minutes ago."

"Dash it, where is he?"

"Last time I looked, he had *my* father buttonholed over by

that tapestry hanging on the far wall. No doubt hashing over that dreadful business of Perceval's murder in the lobby of the House of Commons last month. Things have come to a pretty pass when a madman such as Bellingham feels free to shoot a British prime minister."

"I quite agree," Marcus replied, deciding for the sake of brevity not to elaborate on the subject.

A quick glance proved that the Earl of Fairfax was standing where Bertie suggested, and indeed was engaged in what seemed to be a deep discussion, but with Marcus's mother rather than Mr. Thistlethwaite.

Lady Fairfax was taller than her husband by a good three inches. He had often marveled at his father's self-confidence in choosing such a statuesque bride.

Granted, his mother was a handsome woman, but his father's looks were passable, and, like Marcus's younger brother, John, who took after him both in stature and personality, he possessed a most remarkable smile. His tide and fortune must have afforded him the pick of society's beauties. The same could be said of his mother. As a well-favored and well-dowered young girl, she had not lacked for suitors.

Marcus had long come to the conclusion that where love was concerned, the human heart had no choice. He regretted that his own heart seemed impervious to Cupid's arrows, but such sentiments were quickly put aside when he saw his mother cast a perishing look in his direction.

Lord. That tears it. Mother looks angry enough to rip out my heart and serve it on toast. I completely forgot about Miss Gray. No use worrying about it now, the damage is done.

He returned his attention to Bertie. "I say, old chap, jolly glad to see you of course, but I must confess that you were the last person I expected to see here this evening. Everything all right?"

Bertie nodded to an ebony, silver-handled walking stick propped up against the marble fireplace. "I have been assured that I shall most probably live to a ripe old age, providing I mend my wicked ways, of course. But that is nothing new; the family doctor has been telling me that since our Oxford days."

"I am sure that, given time, we both shall mend our ways. I know that ever since your send-off to the war, I exercise considerably more caution at such functions. I have no wish to suffer any more morning-after consequences of such epic proportions."

"Quite," Bertie rejoined with a rueful smile. "I must confess that I do not recall much of what took place that evening. I must have passed out, because I came to in a cabin on a wretched tub headed for the Peninsula. Haven't the foggiest notion how I got there—do you?"

Marcus grinned. "I believe the credit must go to that batman you took on. Excellent fellow, I might add."

"Ah yes. Knobby is a wonderful chap. A colonel snapped him up as soon as I embarked for home. Quite a step up for Knobby." This remark was followed by a smile that quickly deteriorated into a wince.

"I say, old chap, would you not be better sitting down?" Marcus asked.

"Not really. It would be a trifle hazardous in such a crush. Cannot bend the old knee. Dreadful bore."

"In what battle did you sustain such an injury?"

Looking sheepish, Bertie leaned toward Marcus and whispered, "None that was mentioned in the newspapers. I was dallying in the boudoir of a dark-eyed beauty named Serafina. The jade neglected to mention that she had a very jealous husband who just happened to be a dab hand with a pistol. Need I say more?"

Marcus shook his head. "You paint a vivid picture."

"Thought you would find it interesting." Bertie rubbed his finger down the side of his nose. "I do not wish to alarm you, Marcus, but could your mother have cause to murder you, by any chance? The look she is aiming in your direction is enough to make a chap's blood run cold."

"Oh, oh. I am sorry to cut this short, Bertie, but if I value my life, I must needs engage a certain Miss Gray in polite conversation forthwith."

Bertie regarded him with unholy glee. "Carrying on the Fairfax line must be pure, unmitigated hell."

Marcus inclined his head. "Perhaps. But I am afraid we shall have to postpone this discussion for the nonce. Sanders just entered the room to announce dinner. I had better collect the aforementioned young lady and escort her to her seat. Do you need any assistance?"

Bertie shook his head. "Wouldn't have let my parents talk me into coming if I could not take care of myself. Run along and collect your dinner partner, there's a good fellow."

Later, Marcus tossed and turned in his bed, muttering, "I tried. God knows I tried. What on earth possessed Mother to think that I would be interested in such an insipid girl? Her entire vocabulary consisted of *yes, no,* and *do you really think so?* And that freezing look of hers. Brr! Most disconcerting to say the least."

He groaned, buried his head under the pillows, and continued to fume until sleep took over.

Marcus woke early the next morning. He lay quietly contemplating the blue and silver design of the damask curtains adorning his bed for as long as he could, then threw the bedcovers aside and tugged at the bellpull hanging above the nightstand.

A bleary-eyed Hillman answered the call. "I am dreadfully sorry, sir. I did not realize we were leaving this morning."

"Nor are we."

"My mistake, sir. What with it being so early and all. Why, the household servants have just begun to go about their morning tasks."

"Nevertheless, I wish to get out of my bed and into my clothes as quickly as possible. Dash it, I hate sleeping in four-poster beds. They remind me of coffins."

"Really sir?" Hillman did not elaborate further. "Are you sure you want to rise this early?" he continued. "Perhaps a glass of warm milk would enable you to roll over and go back to sleep. I should be only too happy to go down to the kitchen and get some for you."

"Thank you, but *no*, Hillman. As soon as I am dressed, I intend to take a turn around the gardens before everyone else starts milling about out there. Then perhaps I shall be able to eat my breakfast in peace and quiet The others are not likely to stir for *hours*."

Marcus soon found that his early morning walk left much to be desired. An unusually chilly breeze for June whipped through the trees, and it did not take him long to realize that the jacket he had chosen to wear was inadequate to keep out the cold. By the time he reached the old oak where he had encountered Clarissa Carter, his teeth were chattering, so he turned on his heel and retraced his steps.

He encountered Sanders in the main hallway. The faithful retainer's usually impassive face registered surprise. "My goodness, sir, you must be freezing, venturing forth at this time of day. Thank goodness we have a good fire going in the morning room. Might I suggest that you avail yourself of its warmth?"

"Most assuredly. Some hot tea would also be welcome."

"But of course, sir. Breakfast, too. I shall see that cook is informed immediately." Sanders snapped his fingers, and a footman sitting in a nearby alcove sprang to do his bidding.

As Marcus stood with his back to a crackling fire waiting for his breakfast to be served, he sipped on a dish of steaming hot pekoe tea and savored the pleasures that came with rank and privilege. Granted, his mother was constantly haranguing him to take a wife and settle down, but all in all, he had to admit that life was sweet.

Presently, three footmen entered the room bearing silver domed dishes that they placed on a sideboard, then bowed, and discreetly left the room. The delicious aroma of gammon and eggs mingling with that of freshly baked scones drew Marcus to the sideboard.

While helping himself to generous portions of the food, the telltale creak of a door signaled the arrival of another seeking an early breakfast. *Fine*, he thought *now I shall have to listen to some old bore go on about the weather or, even worse, endure a dissertation on how to win the war.*

With inbred courtesy, he put on his most genial smile and turned to greet his would-be breakfast companion. "Good mor—ning," he said, and silently cursed for having faltered like a stripling at his first ball, for directly at his shoulder stood Miss Gray, regarding him with alarmingly penetrating pale blue eyes.

"Good morning, Lord Ridley," she replied. "I see that you also are given to rising early."

The tone of her voice was aloof, making it clear that she did not care what sort of morning he had, good or bad. Marcus felt affronted. He surveyed the firmly tied lace cap framing her hair, which was the silvery shade of blonde seldom seen on those past infancy.

Pale eyes, pale hair, pale skin. I suppose she is beautiful, but I do not desire her. She is cold and icy. I doubt she would warm a man's bed of a night. There will be no encouragement from this quarter. Lord, I wish my mother would stop meddling in my affairs.

"Please take my plate, Miss Gray. There is plenty more."

"Thank you, but I must decline. I was only looking for a cup of tea."

Marcus pointed to a silver tea service. "The pot contains a pekoe. If it is not to your liking, please say so. There is plenty to choose from in the tea cabinet."

Dianthus Gray shook her head. "That will not be necessary."

She turned down his offer to pour it for her. Upon pouring tea into a delicate bone china cup, she added a generous amount of milk and sugar. Sitting across the table from him, she proceeded to take tiny sips from her teacup, staring at him over the rim as she did so.

Her eyes registered no emotion whatsoever. This made him feel like a butterfly specimen pinned to a board. Completely unnerved, Marcus put down his knife and fork, convinced that he could not down another morsel if his life depended on it.

In an attempt to cut through the atmosphere, he said, "I trust that you are enjoying the weekend? I understand my mother has planned some outdoor activities for this afternoon—providing the sun comes out."

Dianthus put down her teacup. "I find the whole thing to

be completely degrading."

"Really, now? And what 'thing' might that be?"

"You know. This business of the lord and lady of the manor inviting several young ladies for the weekend for their son and heir to inspect like so much breeding stock. I will make it easier for you."

"You will?" Marcus replied guardedly.

She nodded. "Kindly cross me off your list I am not in the least bit interested in marrying you."

Marcus was taken aback. *In that case, you are the first young lady of my acquaintance to take such a stance.*

He was seized with an illogical urge to make her like him, but her next words brought him to his senses.

"It has been my experience that gentlemen as handsome as you are far too enamored of themselves to truly love anyone else."

What an outrageous thing to say! Yet it has a familiar ring. Which among my friends is given to uttering such self-righteous poppycock?

His inner voice responded, *Sounds suspiciously like the drivel you subjected poor Hillman to only last evening.*

Recognizing that he shared at least one of Dianthus Gray's shortcomings did nothing to mitigate the umbrage he directed toward her for the set-down she had so ruthlessly delivered.

"Rest assured, Miss Gray," he said icily, "I do not liken young ladies to brood mares. Even if it means my line dies with me, I would never marry a woman I did not love. I think it is safe to say that you and the rest of the young ladies currently partaking of my parents' hospitality are free to enjoy the rest of the weekend secure in the knowledge that I have no designs upon any of you."

Dianthus shot to her feet, the contents of the teacup spilling into the saucer as she slammed it onto the table. "Well!" she exclaimed, her face turning pink with indignation. Marcus decided that the touch of color did wonders for her complexion.

"Sit down, Miss Gray. You cannot have it both ways."

"I do not know what you mean," she said, while swiftly doing his bidding, the muslin of her dress making a puffing noise as her bottom made contact with the chair seat.

He raised a brow, hoping it would convey his skepticism, got up from the table and inclined his head. "Of a certainty you do. If you will excuse me, I shall leave you to finish your tea in peace."

Once out of the room, he ran the back of his hand across his brow and gave a sigh of relief, aware that he had come dangerously close to being treed.

Dianthus Gray is a new sort of huntress. Wilier and far more deadly than any I have come up against. Not for her the commonplace compromise. A female who pits a man's own vanity and his instinct for the chase against him is far too dangerous to be let loose. She damned near clamped me by the ankle. I must be getting soft in the head.

Deciding it was time to reach the high ground, Marcus took the stairs leading to his chamber two at a time. Once within the cozy confines of his own room, he paced the floor, ruminating over the flaws in his own character that had made him so vulnerable to the machinations of Dianthus Gray.

Chapter 5

Later that morning, the sun broke through the clouds in a blaze of triumph. "Might have known it," Marcus murmured, gazing though his bedroom window.

"Might have known what?" Bertie asked.

"That the sun *would* have to come out." Marcus turned to face Bertie, who was seated by the fireplace batting his walking stick from one hand to the other.

"Great heavens, man, are you going to play with that confounded thing all day? Did you not sustain a nasty bump on your head not five minutes ago trying to catch it in midair?"

"A chap has to do something to pass the time of day." He gave Marcus a quizzical look. "What are you fussing about? I should think you would welcome a little bit of sunshine."

"Because by now, my mother probably has half a dozen footmen scurrying about, setting up nets and unpacking bats and balls while another half dozen are busy hammering Pall Mall hoops into the grass."

"And this is reason to foam at the mouth?"

"I think so. I am the one who will have to spend the better part of the afternoon enduring the company of the frosty Miss Gray and her sister, Primrose."

"Primrose? The one who laughs like a demented peahen?"
Marcus sighed. "One and the same."

"I *was* going to sit on the sidelines and cheer you on, so to speak, but I have to think about it. That laugh could raise the dead."

"Coward. I thought we promised to risk life and limb for one another during our Eton days."

Bertie shrugged. "I promised you my life. My eardrums are

another matter entirely.""

"If you say so."

"I do. By the way, I almost let it slip by, but did I not hear certain hostility in your attitude toward the older Miss Gray? Frosty, indeed. I had the occasion to exchange a few pleasantries with her and found her to be *most* amiable."

"That does not surprise me. She has no designs on you."

Bertie's eyebrows shot up almost to his hairline. "That does not make sense, old chap. Are you feeling all right? Perhaps your mother overdid it. Throwing three females at you in one weekend might have pushed you round the bend."

"Bertie, stop nattering. You are way off the mark."

Marcus told Bertie of Dianthus Gray's cold and calculating nature and the trap she had set for him. He expected Bertie to respond to her perfidy with exclamations of outrage on his behalf, but on hearing the story, Bertie slapped his good leg and howled with glee. Marcus was most put out.

"I am glad you find it amusing," he said stiffly.

"I say, old thing, keep your perspective. I find the little minx most intriguing. Since you have no interest in her, I daresay you will not mind if I pay her court."

Marcus recoiled. "Good lord, Bertie, are you quite mad? That scheming little vixen will lead the poor man who has the misfortune to marry her around by the nose, without him having the slightest notion it is happening."

"But do you not see? I should have splendid fun besting her at her own game. It would afford me a lifetime of diversion."

"One of unmitigated hell, more likely. Tread softly, my friend. Unlike chess, this is a game you could very well lose."

"Do not worry on my account. I shall test the waters first. Who knows? We may not suit at all."

"That will be my fervent prayer. In the meantime, feel free to use the library. My father has several new books on the table in there." He looked through the window once more. "Dash it. People are beginning to trickle onto the lawn. I suppose I had better join them. My mother is cross with me as it is."

Bertie grinned. "I have changed my mind. It may take me

a while to get downstairs, but I would not miss this opportunity for the world."

"Really?"

Bertie nodded. "Miss Gray shall receive all the encouragement I can muster."

"You must have done more damage to your pate with that damned walking stick than I realized."

"Nevertheless," said Bertie, "I am going to make the most of this. You have no idea how bored I have been of late."

It did not take long for Marcus to become thoroughly irked by Bertie's presence on the lawn. It was bad enough that Dianthus Gray proved to be a formidable adversary in the game of Pall Mall, addressing each hoop with ease, without Bertie responding to her victories with vigorous applause and exclamations of, "Oh, I say, well done, Miss Gray!"

For her part, Miss Gray rewarded each of Bertie's extravagant outbursts with a dimpling smile and a gracefully executed curtsy. To make matters worse, she nosed Marcus out of first place by the merest of margins and accepted the congratulations of her fellow participants with an infuriating display of false modesty.

"It was pure chance. I am really not very good at games," she said with a deprecating laugh, while according Marcus a look of triumph.

Marcus would fain have wrapped her mallet around her lovely throat, but feared such an act would incur the wrath of his lady mother. Instead, deciding to get as far away from Miss Gray as possible, he turned down an invitation to play shuttlecock and battledore in favor of taking a stroll around the garden. Miss Gray also begged off, and immediately sat down on the chair next to Bertie's.

As Marcus strode away, he heard her say, "Mr. Thistlethwaite, it was so gallant of you to champion my cause. I am sure you were responsible for my good account at Pall Mall."

Marcus feared for Bertie. He might be up for a game of wits with Dianthus, but would he be able to withstand her flattery? His friend's vanity could well prove to be his downfall, for it would seem that the lady was determined to salvage something from her stay at Fairfax Towers. Bertie was heir to a considerable fortune.

Just when Marcus thought the afternoon could not possibly get any worse, a piping voice called out, "Wait for me, my lord. If you do not mind, I should like to walk with you."

Silently cursing, Marcus turned and waited for Primrose Gray to catch up. Mercifully, Primrose fell into step with him, and walked by his side in silence, sparing him the discomfort of her less than dulcet tones.

Alas, his reprieve was short lived, because on approaching the old oak tree she let forth with a spate of nerve-shattering chatter that almost unmanned him.

At first Marcus was too preoccupied in planning his escape to take in what she was saying, when mention of her sister Dianthus claimed his full attention.

"I absolutely detest her, you know. Dianthus is devious and mean-spirited. She has made my life miserable for as long as I can remember."

Marcus responded with a discreet cough.

"Pah," Primrose responded. "Pray do not adapt that attitude. You do not like her, either."

"You presume too much, young lady."

"Nonsense. You must have sent her packing with a flea in her ear. The atmosphere between the two of you is positively arctic." Primrose giggled. "I told her cornering you in the breakfast room would not do her a bit of good."

Marcus stopped in his tracks directly under the oak. "You have said enough. I think it is high time we returned to the others."

To his dismay, she clutched at his sleeve. He let out a groan. *Please, God, not another lovelorn Bath miss, I beg of you.*

"Lord Ridley, hear me out. Marry me. You will not regret it. I promise I shall devote my whole life to making you happy."

A daunting proposition if ever I heard one.

He pried her fingers from his sleeve. "Primrose, end this right now. I am not unmindful of the honor you bestow upon me, but we do not suit. In the first place, you are far too young. How old are you, child? Fourteen? Certainly no more than fifteen."

"I am sixteen. At least, I shall be next month, and I am very mature for my age."

"Please, say no more. As far as I am concerned, this conversation did not occur. Stay here, if you wish, but I am returning to the others."

"No!"

Her voice was so strident Marcus flinched.

"No! I will *make* you marry me." She punctuated the word *make* with a stamp of her foot.

Marcus shook his head. "It does not work that way, and if you were not such a child, you would know it."

"Would I? If you walk away from me, I shall scream and tear my dress and accuse you of all sorts of unspeakable behavior and you will *have* to do the gentlemanly thing."

"What makes you think that your sordid little scheme will work? Be assured, I am not the gentleman you suppose me to be."

Primrose shrugged. "It will work. That is how my oldest sister, Marguerite, became Baroness Tattenhall."

Marcus grinned. "Hence, poor Tattenhall's hangdog expression. It appears that the Gray sisters make a very poisonous bouquet. Take my word for it Primrose, you would be far happier marrying a man who loves you."

Primrose tugged at her bodice, but the material would not give. She glared at Marcus. "I should warn you, my scream is earth-shattering."

"Why does that not surprise me?"

Without responding, Primrose took a deep breath and closed her eyes. Marcus set off at a brisk walk, hoping to put as much distance as possible between them before she made good on her promise.

He had gone but half a dozen steps when a voice that was far too melodious to be mistaken for Primrose's called out. "Utter one sound, you perfidious creature, and you shall suffer the consequences."

Clarissa? What the devil is she doing here?

Then he heard a rustling of leaves and the ominous tearing of cloth. Thinking to see Primrose's bodice in tatters, Marcus wheeled around in time to see Clarissa swing down from a tree branch, several inches of white lace hanging from beneath her skirt.

Clarissa landed squarely on her feet, surveyed the torn lace, and scowled at Primrose. "Botheration, girl," she muttered, "you are more trouble than you are worth."

Primrose gave her head a haughty toss. "Ladies do not use such language, but then a lady would scarcely wear lace of such shoddy quality, would she?"

Marcus retraced his steps, deeming it politic to gain control of the situation before Primrose subjected Clarissa to any more of her cruel snobbery. He need not have worried.

Primrose received a scornful, "Hah!" from Clarissa, followed by, "There is more to being a lady than the quality of one's lace. But then one who conducts herself in a manner which would make a courtesan blush can hardly be expected to know that, can she?"

Marcus put a hand on Clarissa's shoulder. "Steady on. From this point, Miss Gray is no longer in a position to work her mischief."

He addressed Primrose. "This incident shall be our secret. If I even suspect that you are working your wiles on some other unsuspecting fool, I shall prevail upon Miss Carter to join me in exposing you."

Primrose opened her mouth as if to respond, then clamped it shut.

Marcus waved her away. "Run along now. I shall catch up with you presently. I wish to say a few words to Miss Carter."

As soon as Primrose was out of earshot, he turned to Clarissa. "Did you not promise me that you would not climb the oak again?"

"No."

"No? Clarissa, how can you look me in the eye and deny it?"

"Because it is so. I promised not to let you *catch* me climbing the oak. You would not have, either, if you had not walked into the trap that silly little goose set for you."

"Clarissa, such sophistry is not worthy of you. Besides, I neither asked for nor wanted your help. Miss Gray is not the first young Bath Miss who has tried to compromise me, and I doubt she will be the last. I would risk social ostracism rather than submit to such trickery."

"Silly me. I should have known," Clarissa rejoined, her eyes blazing with anger. "Being so handsome must be a terrible burden. You must be fending off such creatures all day long."

Marcus was affronted. The latest crop of young girls certainly overstepped themselves. What was the world coming to? He was about to give her a thorough set down when it occurred to him that perhaps her sarcasm was well earned.

And delivered with such flair. I should have thanked her for coming to my rescue. When did I become such a pompous ingrate?

He handed her an olive branch. "Forgive me, Clarissa. That was a trifle heavy handed of me, was it not?"

Clarissa's eyes widened in surprise. "Perhaps."

"Let me start over."

Clarissa offered no response.

"First of all, I *am* grateful that you foiled Miss Gray's sordid little scheme. To be honest, it was that business of you breaking your promise to me that set me off. You were always such a forthright little thing."

Clarissa kicked at a grass tuft and then looked him squarely in the eye. "I am sorry for that. I should not have played with the intent of a promise. I am truly ashamed."

"Then you promise not to do it again?"

"Do what again?"

"Why, roam all over Fairfax climbing the trees, of course."

"I am sorry, that is a promise I cannot make."

"Good Lord, Clarissa, you are liable to have the dogs set on you."

Clarissa shrugged. "Your father would not allow it. Neither would you."

Marcus threw up his hands. "I should have known. Once

a gnat, always a gnat. Do not lay it at my door if you break any bones. I wash my hands of you."

Thoroughly exasperated, Marcus was about to take his leave of her when he noticed the forlorn looking scrap of lace trailing from beneath her skirt and across the toe of an extremely scuffed brown leather shoe.

By Jove, surely old Carter can do better than that by his daughter.

Clarissa saw the expression on his face and interpreted it rightly. "I do have others, you know."

"I beg your pardon. I do not follow you."

"Shoes. You were regarding mine with utter disdain. They are good enough for climbing trees. My mother threw them out once, but I was able to retrieve them." She looked at his expression for any sign of disapproval and, seeing none, continued, "I keep them hidden in the shed. If she knew I still had them she would throw a fit."

"And rightly so," Marcus rejoined. "It would seem, young lady, that you live your life from one deception to another. I doubt I ever really knew you."

"Probably not." She softened this remark with an impish little smile that always worked wonders with her father. To her relief, Marcus smiled back.

"We will discuss your shortcomings at a later date. I had better catch up with Miss Primrose Gray before she can stir up more mischief. By the way, I insist on replacing that lace."

Clarissa offered up a silent curse, wishing Primrose Gray off the face of the earth for calling attention to it. "Please do not trouble yourself, Lord Ridley. It would have torn sooner or later. You see, it was salvaged from one of my grandmother's petticoats and is very, very old."

"Nevertheless, it is the least I can do to express my gratitude. I would have dealt with Miss Gray, but your presence certainly saved me from an embarrassing situation."

"You cannot be talked out of it?"

Marcus shook his head. "Point of honor."

"In that case, might I make a request?"

"By all means," he replied.

"It may sound outrageous, and I shall understand if you refuse me."

"For goodness sake, Clarissa, *do* get on with it. How outrageous could it possibly be?"

"I would be most grateful if you could see your way to giving me a pair of your old breeches. Nothing fancy, of course."

"Of course. Are you *mad*, Clarissa? Such a request goes far beyond outrageous. Of what possible use could my breeches be to you?"

"For one thing, they would prevent me from tearing my unmentionables on Fairfax tree branches."

Marcus stroked his chin. Clarissa felt a glimmer of hope. At least he was considering the matter. Then he gave her the most devious smile she had ever encountered, and her heart sank.

"Done," he said.

"Really and truly?" Clarissa grasped his hand and began to pump it. "How very kind of you. I am truly grateful." Suddenly aware of the liberty she had taken, she dropped his hand.

"Do not be too grateful. The offer comes with limitations."
Limitations? That did not bode well.

"I want your word as a lady that you will not climb any trees unless I am here and it is convenient for me to accompany you. It is folly to climb unattended. What if you were to fall? You could lie there for hours."

Clarissa fought the urge to dance a jig. It would be like the old days—almost In those days, she just had worshipped and adored him. Now she was in love with him.

She forced a sigh. "Very well. You have my word."

"I have your word that?"

"That I shall not set foot on Fairfax grounds unless invited."
Clarissa panicked. "You will invite me? This is not just a ruse?"

Marcus stiffened. "The very idea. Of course, do not expect me to oblige you every time I visit Fairfax. I do have social obligations."

"But how shall I know? You cannot very well knock on my door and ask Mama permission to take me tree climbing."

"You know, Clarissa, I am having second thoughts about the

whole thing. All this plotting and deception does not sit well."

Clarissa set her jaw, determined not to let this boon slip through her fingers. "You promised."

"Yes, I did. Let me think." He knitted his brow for a moment, then said, "I have it. When I am here, I shall meet you by stile the day after I arrive."

"When?"

Marcus shrugged. "Morning? Afternoon?"

"Afternoon, about two o' clock? Mama always takes her nap then."

Marcus looked hesitant.

Clarissa prayed he would not change his mind.

"Very well. Wait no longer than ten minutes. I shall do likewise. It is to be hoped that you will soon outgrow this childish predilection for tree climbing. Dashed inconvenient, if you must know."

Clarissa crossed her fingers within the folds of her dress. "I expect I shall."

"Good." He looked across the lawn. "Botheration. It is too late to catch up with that confounded girl. Run along home, Clarissa, before she inveigles both of us into a scandal."

Would that such a scandal existed, Clarissa thought as she dropped Marcus a demure curtsy and took her leave.

Chapter 6

After waving good-bye to the last carriage load of guests to depart, Lady Fairfax lowered her kerchief and said, "This weekend went very well, I must say."

"Quite," Lord Fairfax replied. "A fine trio of young fillies, do you not agree, my boy? Your mother did well by you."

"I am sure that Mother did her best, but I think in future I should be left to choose my own bride."

Lady Fairfax pressed her lips into a thin line. "Apparently, Marcus, you have decided not to like any girl that I might deem suitable."

Marcus shook his head. "That is not the case, Mother. Once we are inside and out of earshot of the servants I shall apprise you of the nightmare this weekend turned out to be for me."

As if on cue, both parents subjected him to riveting stares.

His father was the first to speak. "Pray do not tell me you have got yourself into another coil."

"Not exactly, but it could very well have ended that way."

"Not another word until we get to my sitting room," his mother said. Then, turning on her heel, she entered the house.

Upon hearing Marcus's account of what had transpired that weekend, his parents sat gripping the arms of their chairs in white-knuckled shock. His father was the first to recover.

"That is the most scurrilous thing I have ever heard," he spluttered. "Are you sure you are not mistaken about the older Miss Gray? After all, it is quite possible that not every girl of our acquaintance is taken with you. Not that it matters. The younger girl's behavior puts an end to any dealings we might have had with those people."

"According to Miss Primrose Gray, her sister was waiting to

pounce on me at breakfast. It seems that she made it a point to learn my habits."

"Dreadful family. And to think I was encouraging an alliance with them," Lady Fairfax inserted. "By the way, how did Clarissa Carter happen to be on hand?"

"I could not say for sure. Perhaps she was taking a stroll in the pasture. That ghastly voice of Primrose Gray's carries a distance," Marcus replied, cringing at the lie.

"Soul destroying," his father added with a shudder.

"This is all very well, Marcus," his mother interjected. "But what of the other two young ladies? They are both diamonds of the first water, and both known to be amiable."

"Eleanor Simpson is a good sort, but we would make a dreadful match. She is far too much of a bluestocking to be interested in me, or I her."

"And Sara Haynes? How does she fall short of your lofty standards, pray tell?"

"Play fair, Mother. Lady Sarah is also a nice girl. Far too nice for me, in fact. She has not a thought in her head that has not been drummed there by her strait-laced parents. One could die of ennui married to such a female."

His mother knitted her brow. "Next time I shall give a little more thought to my selection of prospective brides."

Marcus rose from his chair. "I thank you for the effort you put into this weekend, Mother, but I will have no more of this matchmaking nonsense." He bowed to his parents. "Now if you will excuse me, I shall gather up my servants and return to London."

He hesitated at the door. "By the way, Mother, I would be obliged if you would purchase some lace for me on your next trip into the village."

His mother's eyebrows shot up. "Oh? What an odd request. Might I ask what manner of lace you require, how much, and for whom it is intended?"

Marcus shrugged, instantly regretting his decision to foist the task onto her. "The sort of lace that young ladies put on their undergarments, I should imagine. You are the better judge as to how much. Oh—and see that it is of the very finest quality. Miss Carter caught hers on the underbrush coming to my aid."

His mother's eyes widened. "Really, Marcus. The finest lace for young Clarissa? What do you think her parents will make of that?"

Marcus shrugged. "If it comes from you, the Carters will be bowled over by your gracious condescension, I should imagine."

"Marcus, you go too far. I will not help you to further this deception."

"I should hope not," Lord Fairfax interjected. "Young man, scandal seems to dog your heels. Up till now, I have always believed your protestations of innocence. But now I am beginning to wonder."

Marcus felt his hackles rising. "With all due respect, Father, I do not care for the implication. There is nothing untoward in my intent toward Miss Carter. I merely wish to make good on an obligation."

Lord Fairfax frowned. "Marcus, it is most improper. I demand you put an end to this nonsense. It is not fair to lead the girl on."

"I have no intention of leading her on. Miss Carter does not interest me in the slightest, nor I her."

"Are you quite sure?" his mother asked.

"Of course I am. She does not pique my interest one iota. To me, Clarissa will always be that annoying little girl who would not give John or me a moment's peace."

"I was referring to the young lady, not you." Lady Fairfax spoke with the patience usually reserved for the simple minded. "How can you be sure she has not developed a *tendre* for you?"

"Clarissa?" Marcus punctuated her name with a dry laugh. "I doubt it. She does not show the slightest interest in me. But I can see that giving her lace might not be quite the thing."

Lady Fairfax looked relieved. "I am glad that is settled. It would be far more appropriate to invite Clarissa and her mother for afternoon tea. Do you not agree?"

Marcus failed to see how an invitation to tea had any bearing on the subject, but responded with a polite, "Quite. It is very good of you, Mother. I am sure the Carters will benefit from your kind regard."

His mother nodded. "I am of the opinion that the consequence it will afford them will more than make up for the loss of a bit of lace."

"Capital," Marcus replied. "Mother, you can always be trusted to make the right decision. Now if you will excuse me, I shall prepare to leave for London within the hour."

When Mr. Carter returned home from his responsibilities to the Fairfax estate, Clarissa was about to come downstairs to greet him when Mrs. Carter met him at the door shaking with excitement and waving a sheet of cream-colored paper under his nose.

Not wishing to intrude upon her mother's pleasure, Clarissa retreated into the shadows of the upstairs landing.

"I thought you would never get home," Mrs. Carter twittered. "See? It is an invitation. I have been waiting all afternoon to share the good news with you."

Narrowly missing a poke in the eye by the heavy bond paper, he held his wife at arm's length. "From the way you are carrying on, I presume we have been asked to dine at Buckingham Palace."

Mrs. Carter pulled the paper back and pouted. "Now you have spoiled it for me."

Mr. Carter put his arm around her shoulder. "That was not my intention, my dear," he said. He led her into the drawing room. "The light is better in here. Perhaps you will be so kind?" He held out his hand.

She placed the letter in it. "It is an invitation for Clarissa and me to take tea with her ladyship next Tuesday."

Mr. Carter read it, then regarded his wife over the top of his glasses. "So it would seem. Then I need not worry about shaking the moths out of my evening clothes. Just as well. They are probably hopelessly out of date."

"I should imagine they are," Mrs. Carter responded tartly.

"Electing to become another man's steward did nothing for our social standing."

Mr. Carter frowned and handed the invitation back to her. "Do not refine on the matter, Beatrice. You knew when you accepted my offer of marriage that neither the clergy nor the army held any appeal for me, and I enjoy my work. Lord Fairfax pays me a generous stipend and has provided us with a stout roof over our heads."

Clarissa clenched her hands. *Will Mama never learn to hold her tongue?*

Wishing to save her father from further criticism, Clarissa bounded down the stairs and entered the living room.

Her mother looked toward the door and frowned. "Really, Clarissa, even a ploughboy shows better grace. It is to be hoped that you do not bring shame on our family while taking tea with Lady Fairfax next Tuesday."

Clarissa dropped her mother a curtsy. "I am sorry. In my haste to share the good news with Papa, I quite forgot. It shall not happen again."

"There's a good girl," her mother replied.

Mr. Carter ruffled Clarissa's hair. Then, taking a folded newspaper out of his pocket, he took his favorite seat by the fire and opened it up.

"It is very good of his lordship to pass on his newspapers to you," Mrs. Carter's said, her voice dripping honey.

Mr. Carter's only response to this provocation was an impatient rustling of his newspaper.

Mrs. Carter brushed imaginary dust off the mantelpiece with her forefinger. "Thank goodness Clarissa extended the hem of her cream-colored afternoon dress with the band of pale blue I was able to salvage from one of my old dresses. She has done an admirable job of the pin-tucking and quilling."

Mr. Carter looked up from his newspaper. "Really? How gratifying. I had no idea she had the patience for such work."

"It is a skill she acquired while staying at your brother's house. Now if you will excuse me, I shall go see how your dinner is coming along. You will be pleased to hear that we are having strawberries and clotted cream for a sweet."

Mr. Carter's face visibly brightened. "Really? I had no idea that the strawberries were even close to being ripe."

Mrs. Carter patted his shoulder. "They are not, dear. They are from one of the Fairfax hothouses. They came with the invitation to tea." She gave an excited little giggle. "Edwin. I have a good feeling about this. Do you suppose that Lady Fairfax finally realizes that I am a cut above the other ladies in the parish? I am sure that a true aristocrat has an eye for such things."

"It is quite possible." Mr. Carter responded dryly. "In the meantime, oh light of my life, try not to pin all of your hopes on such an eventuality."

Chapter 7

Ever since his return to the family town house in Mayfair, Marcus was plagued by a vague discontent. That had been in June. It was now the middle of July, and the rain thrumming against the withdrawing room windows made him feel as restless as a caged animal.

He cast a jaundiced eye on Bertie, who was nodding off in front of the hearth in the armchair directly facing his. For lack of something better to do, Marcus jabbed at the logs burning in the hearth, causing the flames to roar and spark up the chimney.

This piece of folly earned him Bertie's full attention. "I say. Steady on there, old chap. It would not do to set the chimney on fire."

"At least it would give us a little diversion. If only the rain would stop, we could take the curricle for an airing, or at least go to Boodles." Marcus returned the poker to its stand. "Anything would be better than huddling around this fire like a couple of toothless dotards."

"I would challenge you to a game of billiards, but this damp weather is playing hob with my leg. A game of cards, perhaps?"

Marcus heard the strain in Bertie's voice and saw the white, pinched look around his lips and nostrils. It occurred to him that far from falling asleep, Bertie's eyes had been closed because of the discomfort he suffered.

"You are in no condition to play cards." Marcus got out of his chair and hovered over him. "Surely there is something I can do for you, old chap. Summon a doctor, perhaps?"

Bertie gave him a dismissive wave. "Stop fussing, Marcus. As soon as the weather clears I shall be all right. It is the inactivity I am forced to endure that is driving me round the bend."

"Surely your father can put you to use. You Thistlethwaites own one of the largest estates in Cornwall."

Bertie shook his head. "Out of the question. My father will not let loose of the reins and has no respect for my opinions. I cannot work under such conditions."

"Sounds familiar. That is why I chose to make myself useful to our prince regent. For some reason, he values my judgment. I spend half my life poring over his plans for remodeling either Carlton House or that confounded Pavilion in Brighton."

Bertie looked arch. "Not to mention other affairs of a more sinister nature."

Marcus pretended ignorance. "I cannot imagine what you mean by that."

"That story you put out about your brother John haring all over India, exploring ancient temples and hunting tigers with a maharaja."

"What about it? John had a remarkable time."

"I do not doubt that for one minute. But not in India. Right about the time you placed him at Punjab, I saw him rowing out to a small trading vessel anchored in Camberly Bay."

"A case of mistaken identity."

Bertie shook his head. "Come now, your secret is safe with me. I think this is the reason you did not join the rest of us in Spain. You are involved in some sort of espionage, and I wish to be a part of it."

Marcus hesitated before responding.

Bertie is an honorable man, without a doubt loyal to crown and country. But in his present condition, I fail to see how he can be of help. On the other hand, perhaps the possibility of such an eventuality might speed up his recovery.

"Very well, I give up. But it is not as exciting as you think. You would be a courier, nothing more."

"I am thinking that John's part in this involved more than running errands."

"Perhaps, but the French got wind of it and we had to shut down that sphere of activity."

"But—"

"Sorry, Bertie. It is courier work—or nothing."

Bertie sighed. "Very well, anything for a change. When do I start?"

"Not so fast. First you have to do something about your leg."

Bertie bridled. "Oh? What do you have in mind—amputation?"

Marcus wondered if he could finish what he had to say before his friend got in a good whack with his walking stick. He walked over to the window to put as much distance between them as possible. "A month or two taking the waters at Bath. Soak and swim in the hot water every day until you look like a prune, if that's what it takes. Work that leg to the limit, otherwise the muscles are going to shrivel up."

"A month or two among rheumatic-ridden beldames and gouty old men? You drive a hard bargain, my friend."

Marcus turned away from the window. "Come now, it is not that bad. Bath will be thronging with young beauties this time of year."

Bertie visibly brightened. "Yes, it will."

"Good. Then may I presume that you did not follow through with that little encounter you had with a certain Miss Gray?"

Bertie grinned. "You may. I called on her a time or two, but quickly lost interest. A cunning mind was not the only thing she had in common with a cobra. She lacked a certain warmth."

"You have no idea how relieved I am to hear that, Bertie old chap. I have reason to believe that the whole family is nothing but a nest of vipers. You will be going to Bath, then?"

"I suppose so. I am in need of a little diversion. Care to join me in my misery?"

Marcus grimaced. "How could I refuse? You make it sound so enticing."

"Then you will accompany me?"

Marcus shook his head. "I leave for Brighton tomorrow. Prinny wants to show off some new objet d'art he has acquired so he is having a soiree."

"I do not envy you, old chap. His taste is so bizarre."

Marcus looked rueful. "Without a doubt. Although I must

confess that on a dreary day, and Lord knows we get plenty of those, I find all that color he leans toward quite cheery."

"Harrumph. Then I shall see you within the week?"

"More like two. I plan to visit both Fairfax and Camberly along the way."

Bertie's eyes widened. "But it will be your third or fourth visit to Fairfax since early spring. Your parents are going to get sick of the sight of you if you keep it up."

"That is the best part of belonging to a family. The poor devils are obliged to make one welcome."

"My goodness, Marcus, you sound as if you are actually looking forward to going there."

"I am," Marcus replied, surprised to realize that he meant it.

Marcus arrived at Fairfax Towers early the next afternoon and, knowing that his mother could usually be found there that time of day, headed straight for her sewing room.

As was her habit, his mother was seated next to the window to take advantage of the light, her back to the door. She did not turn to acknowledge his presence, but kept her head bowed over some saffron colored material spilled over her white muslin skirt.

Wonder why I never noticed how gracefully Mother's head sits upon her neck before? Hold on, that is not Mother. Those are red curls beneath that cap. What the devil?

"Clarissa?"

Clarissa jerked her head in his direction and the material draping her lap slipped to the floor with the telltale rustle of taffeta. Marcus hastened to retrieve it at the same time she stood up and bobbed to acknowledge his presence. As he straightened to hand it to her, they bumped heads. Clarissa landed on her bottom and let out a yowl.

Manfully ignoring the pain, which radiated from the bridge of his nose, Marcus dropped her needlework and, grasping her by both hands, unceremoniously hauled her to her feet. On releasing her, he put a solicitous arm around her shoulder.

"Are you all right?"

Clarissa wriggled out of his grasp, her face fast turning pink.

"Quite," she replied, running her hand over the back of her dress.

"You did not *sound* all right."

"Did I not? It must have been the shock. I am perfectly fine." The frantic look she gave him belied her words.

"There is no need to play the stoic. You yelped like a puppy whose paw has been stepped on. Why are you fiddling with the back of your dress?"

The pink in her face turned scarlet. "If you *must* know, my lord, there is a sewing needle sticking into my, um, person, and I would be much obliged if you would leave that I may attend to it."

Marcus fought the urge to laugh. "So that is the seat of your problem? Allow me."

To Clarissa's consternation, he twirled her around, cried, "Aha!" and deftly removed the source of her embarrassment. He handed her what was now a hopelessly bent needle.

Her embarrassment forgotten, she regarded it with dismay. "Oh dear. It is quite ruined. What will Lady Fairfax say?"

"Some words expressing relief that you sustained no lasting hurt, I should imagine."

"I think not. My mother would never let me hear the end of it." She held the needle up. "It is a *beading* needle. Have you any idea how much one of those things costs?"

Marcus shook his head. "Cannot say as I do. But I doubt she will be forced to sell her diamond tiara to pay for it. Do not give it another thought, Clarissa."

Clarissa was too anxious to appreciate his humor. "But—"

"No buts. I accept full responsibility for the mishap. After all, I did startle you. Now not another word."

"Thank you," she said. This was followed by an awkward silence. Clarissa fought the urge to fidget. She wished he would leave, so that she could search the sewing basket for another needle, in order to continue with her work. To add to her discomfort, Marcus regarded her with a quizzical stare.

Finally, Marcus broke the silence. "Tell me, Clarissa, what on earth are you doing here?"

"Sewing for her ladyship, of course."

"Let me rephrase that. *Why* are you sewing for my mother? Her abigail is up to the task."

"She invited Mama and me to take tea with her some time ago, admired the alterations I had made to my dress, and graciously asked me to do some work for her."

Clarissa bent down and retrieved the saffron taffeta from the parquet floor. She held it up for his inspection, and awaited his reaction. As he beheld the intricate cutwork with lace inserts which were in the process of being reembroidered with seed pearls, his expression went from amazement to admiration.

"You did all of that?"

Clarissa nodded. "I am remodeling one of her ladyship's ball gowns. This panel is to be added to the front."

Marcus stroked his chin. "You amaze me. I should have thought you would lack the patience for work of such delicacy."

Clarissa was not sure this remark warranted a thank you, so chose not to offer one.

"Please do not scowl. I meant it as a compliment."

Clarissa felt the heat of embarrassment. She had not intended to show him that she cared one way or the other.

"That is very good of you, I am sure," she replied stiffly. "Now I must beg your indulgence. I promised her ladyship I would finish this before I leave."

Marcus bowed. "In that case, I shall take up no more of your time."

As the door closed after him, it occurred to Clarissa that no mention had been made of meeting her at the stile the following afternoon. Indeed, why should he?

Under the oak tree it had seemed not unreasonable that Marcus would indulge her whims, but within the walls of Fairfax Hall, she was painfully reminded of the gulf separating them.

"I must have been mad," she muttered, jabbing the needle into the taffeta. "Absolutely utterly raving *mad.*"

Even as she uttered these words, Clarissa knew that nothing short of an act of God would stop her from being at the stile well before the appointed hour.

Chapter 8

On leaving the sewing room, Marcus paused for a moment and pondered his encounter with Clarissa. Needlework was the least likely avocation he would have expected of her.

He intended to go up to his chamber, but as he mused over this hitherto unsuspected facet to Clarissa's character, his mother's voice intruded upon his thoughts.

"Marcus, darling," she trilled from halfway up the grand staircase, "I thought I heard you arrive. Why are you standing there in a daze? No matter," she added with a dismissive wave and came down to join him. She offered him her cheek for the expected kiss. "Come walk with me. It is lovely outside, and the roses are blooming in spite of the rain we have had."

Lady Fairfax proceeded to put on the broad-brimmed chip straw hat which she carried and secured it under her chin with ribbons of watered silk. Marcus noticed that the bow she had tied was the same deep shade of blue as her eyes and was moved to compliment her.

"You should wear blue more often, Mother. It becomes you."

"How sweet of you to say so, darling," she replied, sounding both surprised and pleased.

Good lord, he thought, *am I so stingy with compliments?*

"Not at all, Mother," he offered by way of atonement for past neglect. "I mean it from the heart, and I shall be delighted to walk with you. A stroll will feel good after being on horseback for the last couple of hours."

He offered her his arm, and they went out into the garden, Lady Fairfax regaling Marcus with the latest in village gossip along the way.

After admiring and sniffing several of the roses to please

her, Marcus led her to a garden bench and suggested sitting down, "to fully appreciate their beauty," as he put it. Once seated, he mentioned his encounter with Clarissa.

"In heaven's name, Mother, what induced you to let her sew for you?"

"Why would I not? Her work is beautiful."

"But it is demeaning for her to sew for others."

"Nonsense. Besides, she refuses to accept payment for it."

"Mother, I find that shocking. It is not like you to take advantage of others."

Lady Fairfax looked hurt. "You misjudge me. Instead of money, I intend to make her a gift of materials sufficient to provide her with a suitable wardrobe."

"Which would entail?"

She shrugged. "Nothing elaborate. A simple little evening dress for the odd ball or two, a costume for carriage rides, that sort of thing."

"Mother, you must be joking. When will Clarissa go to a ball, for instance?"

"When I invite her to attend one of ours."

Marcus got up from the bench and faced his mother. "That would be cruel. Clarissa is ill-equipped to move in polite society."

"It would be far better for the poor child if that were so." Lady Fairfax sighed. "Unfortunately, her foolish mother sent her to live with her father's brother in Derbyshire for several years. It seems that the gentleman is plump in the pocket and provides his daughters with an excellent governess. Mrs. Carter saw to it that Clarissa was put under her tutelage."

"But to what end?" Marcus demanded, pacing back and forth in front of the bench. "As I see it, Clarissa has been consigned to a cruel limbo. She has been rendered unsuitable for association with her own kind and will be most assuredly shunned by ours. What was her mother thinking?"

She smiled wryly. "That she could marry Clarissa off to your brother John?"

"A steward's daughter?"

"Stranger alliances have been made. The Carters may not

be our social equals, but they spring from respectable, middle-class stock. Mr. Carter is not a mere house steward. By virtue of a sound education, he manages this whole estate for your father, and is paid accordingly."

Marcus stopped pacing. "You sound as if you condone such marriages."

Lady Fairfax eyed him coolly. "Do not be obtuse, Marcus. Just because I acknowledge that such things happen does not mean that they do so with my approval."

"Then why in heaven's name do you intend to thrust Clarissa among her betters?"

"Because there is always an exception to the rule."

Marcus sat down once more. "I cannot imagine what it might be, but I am sure you are about to tell me."

"A widower who already has an heir? Such have been known to overlook the lack of fortune in a second wife, especially a young one. Lancelot Thurgood will do quite nicely, do you not agree?"

"No, I do not," Marcus snapped. "Why would you want to shackle Clarissa to a man old enough to be her father? Lancelot Thurgood must be at least forty."

"That does not signify. Such an alliance would provide Clarissa with a secure place in society, and you may be sure that our kind, gentle Mr. Thurgood would accord her every kindness and consideration."

"Why do you concern yourself with Clarissa?"

"Most days I join her in the sewing room, and I have become quite fond of her. She is a forthright girl without being overbearing, and I find it quite refreshing. Most girls her age try to impress me with glowing accounts of their virtues—I rather suspect in the fond hope I shall recommend them to you."

"You poor darling," Marcus rejoined. "It must be a dreadful bore, but hardly an excuse for meddling in Clarissa's affairs."

Lady Fairfax gestured with both hands. "What are her choices? Governess to another woman's children? Taking in sewing while doomed to live her life out as spinster? And what is worse, doing so under the thumb of that overbearing mother of hers? In comparison, marriage to Mr. Thurgood would be a veritable paradise."

"I doubt she would agree with you. Tread carefully, Mother. One gets little thanks for meddling in the affairs of others."

The following afternoon, Clarissa arrived at the stile a full ten minutes before the church clock struck two. Every waking hour since encountering Marcus in his mother's sewing room, Clarissa had agonized as to whether he would keep their appointment.

At ten minutes after two she was debating the feasibility of waiting any longer when the sight of the long-legged, well-muscled young viscount striding across the meadow caused her heart to leap. She climbed over the stile and walked toward him. As they drew nearer, the sight of a brown sack tucked under his arm elated her. *He had kept his promise!*

"Good afternoon, Clarissa. Sorry to keep you waiting," he said when they drew close, and handed her the sack. "Here are the breeches I promised you. I have a feeling we shall both live to regret this foolishness, but a promise is a promise."

"Thank you. You are most kind, your lordship." Clarissa's voice was hesitant. Now that she actually held the sack within her grasp, she felt a rush of unease. *I must be mad for making such an outrageous demand, and he even madder for humoring me.*

"Oh for goodness sake, Clarissa, dispense with the honorifics—at least when others are not present. We have called each other by our first names far too long for such nonsense."

Clarissa expected to see the impatient tone of his voice reflected in his eyes, but they sparkled with good humor. "Very well, Marcus." She opened the sack, pulled out a length of rope, and gave him a questioning look.

"That is to tie around your waist. To hold up the breeches?"

"I see." Clarissa felt her face flush with heat. Suddenly the likelihood of ever donning his breeches seemed remote.

"You do not have to go through with it, Clarissa. It is quite all right to change your mind."

"Nonsense," she said, stoutly. "I just need to try them on at home. See what adjustments have to be made."

"A wise decision, to be—"

Marcus stopped in mid sentence, his eyes widening. "Great heavens, Clarissa, run toward the stile as fast as you can. Attila has been set among the cows."

"Attila?"

Marcus grabbed her arm and began to run, dragging her behind him. "No time to explain. Run like the devil. He is the meanest, biggest bull you are ever likely to encounter, and he is headed in our direction."

Like Lot's wife, Clarissa had to see for herself. One glimpse of the enraged bovine quickly gaining on them was all it took to lend wings to her feet. Even though laden with the sack, which she clutched in her other hand, she was soon abreast of Marcus. He let go of her arm and stepped back a pace, allowing her to forge ahead.

On reaching the stile, Clarissa threw the sack over to a grassy verge on the other side. She put a foot on the stile to follow when, to her mortification, Marcus speeded the process with a boost to her bottom. He then joined her with a well-executed vault.

In spite of the damp from recent rains, they lay side by side in the grass, panting from exertion. Marcus was the first to regain his breath.

"Well done, Clarissa. I have never seen a girl run so well."

She accorded him a wry smile. "I doubt you have ever seen one being chased by an angry bull before. It is bound to make a difference."

He returned her smile and said, "I cannot agree. Most girls lack your stamina. Besides, you run with the speed and grace of a gazelle. I was hard put to keep up with you."

Clarissa wondered how it would feel to be kissed by such generously curved lips, then had the grace to feel remorse for thinking such a thing. Hoping Marcus did not notice the effect he had on her, Clarissa quickly changed the subject. "Whose idea was it to replace Cecil with that dreadful Attila?"

"Your father's."

Clarissa grimaced. "I prefer Cecil."

Marcus shrugged. "Cecil enjoyed a good chase as well as the next bull."

"But he gave up sooner. I suppose it was his age."

"Cecil *was* getting quite long in the tooth. That is why your father decided it was time for a replacement. Though I am not sure that Attila should be it."

"I, on the other hand, have no doubt whatsoever." Clarissa rejoined. "He is far too dangerous. Sometimes the village children fish in the stream running through the west side of the meadow. I shudder to think of the consequences if this Attila should happen upon them."

"Oh? The little devils are poaching and trespassing, are they? The gamekeeper had better pull up his socks."

Clarissa regretted the need for betraying the children. "Can you not leave him out of this? Surely catching a few tiddlers in homemade nets does no harm, and Mr. Lane is liable to deal harshly with the children. Heaven knows the poor little things have few pleasures."

"Now you are being mawkish. I am sure a set down by Lane is preferable to being gored by a bull. The villagers have to be warned. However, I promise you that the children will not be punished this time."

Clarissa felt a rush of relief. "I am so glad. I should hate to think they would suffer because of me."

Marcus looked thoughtful. "Being a nonconformist, I suppose it is only natural you would sympathize with those imps. Which reminds me, the warning also applies to you, young lady. Keep away from that field—at least until the cattle are moved."

"They are going to be moved?"

"Over to the north pasture some time next month. This field is going to be plowed in readiness for next spring. It has lain fallow long enough."

Before Clarissa could respond, the church clock struck half past two. She was surprised that half an hour had passed so quickly.

Marcus stood up. "I had better be off." He offered her a

hand, but she sprang to her feet of her own volition.

"I should go home too," Clarissa replied, secretly disappointed that he had not stayed longer.

Marcus bid Clarissa good-bye and took off down the lane with his characteristic stride. This route added an extra half mile to his return home, but it was safer than haring across the meadow with the irascible Attila breathing at his back.

Clarissa watched his departure and wondered if he would return before the haying. Once he had disappeared around the hedgerow, she picked up the sack and returned home, her own steps slow and disconsolate.

Chapter 9

A plump housekeeper, tightly encased in a dress of black bombazine, ushered Marcus into the library of the elegant residence the Thistlethwaites owned on the Royal Crescent in Bath. Bertie hobbled across the room to greet him.

"It is good to see you, old chap. Thought you would never get here," he said, while subjecting Marcus to a playful punch to the shoulder.

Marcus took a step backward. "You must be feeling better. That is quite a blow you deliver."

Bertie grimaced. "You think so? Quite frankly, I think this business with the baths is an utter waste of time."

"But you have dispensed with the walking stick."

"I suppose I have. It was too much trouble. Kept leaving it everywhere."

Marcus was about to point out that for this to happen, his need for a walking stick must have lessened, but thought better of it. Bertie was in too much of a funk to listen to reason.

"Been making the rounds, have you?" Marcus offered on the off chance some social engagement might have been to Bertie's liking.

"The odd visit to the lower rooms. The upper ones are too much of a crush. Visited the card room once, and left several hundred guineas the poorer. There is the daily soak in the baths followed by the inevitable trip to the Pump Room to partake of the waters, which, incidentally, taste positively putrid."

To Marcus's relief, Bertie paused to take a breath.

"I *did* go to the theater once. I found it a bore. In my opinion, everything about Bath is bloody boring. Shall I continue?"

"Not on my account. Though I would not turn down a

glass of that brandy," Marcus replied, gesturing toward a table filled with glasses and decanters.

Bertie started. "Forgive me. I was so busy voicing my complaints I quite forgot my duties as host."

"That was not complaining, Bertie."

"Oh?"

"More like whining, and I wish you would stop it. All this sniveling serves no purpose. We are going to enjoy our stay here whether you like it or not. Now pour me that damned drink."

Bertie opened his mouth as if to deliver a rebuttal, then snapped it shut and limped over to the table and filled two large goblets with the amber liquid.

Sitting by the window, Bertie and Marcus relaxed with their feet resting on ottomans and sipped their brandy. Finally Bertie mellowed, and his mood became expansive.

"It is a little Spartan around here right now," he said, sounding more cheerful. "Skeleton staff and all that, but the rest of the family will be here within the week, along with a whole entourage of servants, so things will get better. At least the meals should improve."

"In the meantime, let us make the most of our stay," Marcus inserted. "We do not *have* to make the social round if you find it irksome. We can take excursions into the country. Stop at an inn? Quaff some ale?"

Bertie actually smiled. "Yes. There is a curricle in the carriage house we can use. It is not quite up to scratch, but will suffice."

"There, you see? We shall fare splendidly."

"We had better make the most of it. When my sister arrives she will expect us to escort her to an assembly or two."

"Good lord, is Arabella old enough for those things already? It does not seem possible."

"Nevertheless. By the way, not to change the subject," Bertie said, doing exactly that, "I have not seen your name mentioned in the newspapers since that duel you fought with Edgerton last winter. Nothing to report?"

"Nothing much. Although I did have a narrow escape a couple of weeks ago."

"Another run-in with a jealous husband?"

"No. A bad-tempered bull, as a matter of fact."

By this time, Marcus had made inroads on a second glass of brandy, and, more relaxed than usual, he told Bertie all about his and Clarissa's encounter with Attila, including his reason for being there in the first place.

Bertie's eyes widened with shock. "Did I hear you aright? You not only were unchaperoned, but you were indelicate enough to gift the gel with a pair of your old breeches? I say, old boy, that is outside of enough even for *you.*"

"I expect so, but Clarissa *did* extricate me from that sticky situation with the Gray chit and in a moment of weakness, I promised them to her."

"We are talking about *that* girl? The one who almost killed you by landing on your breadbasket last April? And now because of an ill-considered promise you made to her, a bull almost gored you?" Bertie shook his head. "Avoid her like the plague, my friend, lest you do not survive another encounter."

August was almost over, and Marcus had yet to return to Fairfax Towers. Clarissa did not have to wonder as to his whereabouts. The newspaper her father brought home every evening kept an assiduous record of every move he made.

In Bath, it seemed the main topic of conversation was as to whether "the hitherto confirmed bachelor, Lord R., will offer for a certain Miss T." It seemed that not only was "the fair-haired young beauty" the only young lady with whom the lord deigned to dance at the assemblies, he was also included in her family's party at all other social functions.

The thought of Marcus proposing marriage to another girl, especially one described in such flattering terms, plunged Clarissa into the depths of despair.

I knew it would happen one day. Spending time with Marcus will be out of the question. Was even one afternoon too much to hope for?

Clarissa was disconsolate until later in the week she read in the newspaper words to the effect that "the apparently love-shy Lord R." had fled to London and was keeping the gossip mills busy with accounts of driving his curricle all over town, accompanied by a titian-haired beauty of a "certain age."

"Celeste Markham?" Clarissa cried out. "Surely his brother's marriage to her daughter put an end to that liaison?"

For shame! For all you know, Marcus's friendship with Lady Camberly could be as innocent as the one he shares with you.

"But of course, it is not difficult to believe that Marcus would seek the same sort of friendship with a beautiful, sophisticated widow that he conducts with a gangly girl scarcely out of the schoolroom," Clarissa murmured. "That is, if one wishes to believe it badly enough."

All the same, it behooves one to give a friend the benefit of the doubt.

Clarissa tossed the newspaper onto the hearth. "I must be quite mad. What makes me presume that anyone as lofty as Lord Ridley would deign to number me among his friends?"

Suddenly the living room door creaked open and her mother walked in, bringing Clarissa's conversation with the little voice in her head to an abrupt end.

"Just as I thought," Mrs. Carter said with a frown. "You are talking to yourself again. Clarissa, you really ought to control that tendency. Others are going to think you are a little off."

"And perhaps they would be right," Clarissa replied, feeling thoroughly wretched at the thought.

Mrs. Carter pursed her lips. "I will not tolerate such impertinence."

"I am sorry, Mama. I did not mean to be impertinent."

Clarissa held her breath, hoping that her apology had cooled her mother's displeasure.

"Humph. That is all very well, but in future, I suggest that you weigh your words more carefully."

Clarissa exhaled, thinking that was the end of the matter, when she saw her mother's glance dart to the crumpled newspaper on the hearth.

"Really, Clarissa, such slovenliness will not be tolerated. Pick up that newspaper and put it back on the table in the same condition in which you found it."

Clarissa complied, all the time conscious of her mother's tight-lipped disapproval.

"Now go to the kitchen and make yourself useful to Mrs. Gates. Papa will be home shortly and should not be expected to wait for his dinner."

Eager to escape her mother's displeasure, Clarissa dropped a curtsy and hurried to the kitchen. Mrs. Gates was stirring the contents of an iron kettle on the fireplace hob. She turned and gave Clarissa a welcoming smile.

"Ah, Clarissa. Enjoy your walk, dear? I had hoped you would pop in for a chat when you got back."

"I stopped to read Papa's newspaper. It was full of the usual malicious gossip. I rather think that being a person of no consequence has its advantages."

"I have always thought so. The way they malign our poor Lord Ridley is a disgrace. By the way, that reminds me. When Horace went to the farm to get the milk, he met him coming out of the piggery. His lordship was gracious enough to inquire after his health and that of everyone else's in the Carter household." Mrs. Gates put her hand to her bosom. "Fancy that. A gentleman of his consequence, condescending to speak to the lowliest of servants."

"I do not find that surprising. Lord Ridley is not in the least puffed up," Clarissa replied. "I wonder what he was doing in the piggery. One does not expect that of a gentleman."

"Horace had the temerity to ask, and you may be sure I gave that lad proper telling off for not remembering his place. The very idea!"

"What was his answer?"

"It seemed that while taking a walk, Lord Ridley was overcome by a stench coming from the pig wallow. He was of the opinion that the only solution was to fill it in and dig a new one somewhere else."

Clarissa winced. "Ouch! Mr. Finch would not have taken kindly to that. Papa says he is too touchy by half."

"Your papa is far too charitable. I have known Samuel Finch since we were both in leading strings, and he has always been a spiteful, mean-spirited excuse for a human being."

"Really? Then it is just as well that he is not in a position to do his lordship any harm, do you not agree?"

"Absolutely. Now be a dear and shell those peas, if you will. They are young and tender, just the way your papa likes them."

Chapter 10

Marcus arrived at the stile ahead of Clarissa. While waiting for her, he watched several noisy sparrows peck at ripe rose hips on the briers tangling between the hawthorn and honeysuckle growing in the hedgerow. But their antics did not hold his attention for long, and he grew impatient waiting for her.

He was about to turn heel when he saw Clarissa rounding the bend in the lane. He watched her approach. Her graceful stride gave a rhythmic sway to the flounce embellishing the hem of her dress. Most girls he knew took short, mincing steps. *She is like a filly not quite ready to be taken from her dam*, he thought.

"Terribly sorry I am late," she said when she reached the stile. "Have you been waiting long?"

"Long enough to have taken root, I fear."

"Oh dear," she replied, her forehead knitted with concern. "It could not be helped. Mama was in a talkative mood and showed no sign of being the least bit sleepy. I thought she would never go up for her nap."

"Calm down, Clarissa. It was supposed to be a joke."

"I am such a ninnyhammer," she said, smiling.

He was fascinated to see that the right side of her mouth curved higher than the left, causing a crescent-shaped dimple to form on the lower part of her cheek. Disconcerted for having noticed, he decided to change the subject.

"I see you decided against wearing the breeches. That is a relief."

She hesitated for a moment, and then sheepishly raised the hem of her dress to give him the merest glimpse of his cast-off clothing. "Sorry to disappoint you. But I promise to keep these things hidden from public view. Why would you think otherwise?"

"Clarissa, I do not mean to hurt your feelings, but why would I not? After all, how many young ladies do you imagine share your interest in climbing trees?"

Clarissa could hardly tell him that she had long outgrown her penchant for climbing trees and only climbed the old oak on the off chance of seeing him. "That is hard to tell," she finally replied. "How many have you taught?"

Marcus gave her a reproving glance. "We came here to climb trees, not bandy words." He pointed to a nearby elm. "How about that one for starters?"

Clarissa nodded.

Marcus pointed out to her the branches on the tree he thought they should use to effect their climb. "Mind you, no trying to reach the top—at least not the first time or two."

Clarissa hesitated before tucking the front of her dress into the rope securing the breeches. She studied his face for any sign of disapproval, but he seemed not in the least perturbed.

She found that climbing the elm presented a much greater challenge than the accommodating old oak and was out of breath by the time they were halfway up. It did not help matters that Marcus seemed not the least bit bothered by the climb.

She was greatly relieved when he straddled the branch directly above her and said, "This is high enough for the first day."

Clarissa climbed onto the branch next to his and leaned against the elm's broad trunk for support, painfully aware of her labored breathing.

"My apologies for not noticing, Clarissa, but you are all puffed out. We did not have to climb so high. Why did you not say something?"

"And miss the view up here? Look to the west. One can see the vicarage, and there is the vicar, Mr. Halliwell, talking to one of the parishioners at the garden gate."

"The view notwithstanding, given the circumstances it would not have been untoward for you to beg off."

"What circumstances might they be?" Clarissa's tone was defensive.

"No need to raise your hackles. Tell me this, Clarissa: am I right in assuming that once John joined me at Eton, your tree climbing came to an end?"

"Yes. Mama would not let me out of her sight. I thought I should go mad. But how did you know?"

"It is only natural. She thought you were safe with John and me." This was followed by a wicked laugh. "Had she known about our tree climbing, or perhaps worse yet, the log balancing over the trout stream, she would no doubt have seen to it that John and I were soundly thrashed, and heaven knows what she would have done to you."

"Probably have locked me in my room until I attained my majority."

Marcus gave a short laugh, then looked somber. "And she would have been justified—even more so today. Look, Clarissa, I feel it is dishonorable for us to deceive your parents in such a fashion. We are not children anymore. I would be much obliged if you would release me from my ill-considered promise."

Clarissa could not breathe, much less respond. *For goodness sake, pull yourself together. Say something. Say anything you ninnyhammer.* The mixture of concern and pity in his eyes moved her to speak.

"But of course. That dreadful encounter with Miss Gray caught us both off balance. Otherwise I am quite sure neither of us would have agreed to such a foolhardy scheme."

"It probably had something to do with it. But to be honest, Clarissa, I rather liked the idea of climbing trees with you. I wish you were a boy. Even when you were a little girl, you were always up for any adventure."

As Marcus sounded the death knell to their friendship, Clarissa knew that the sight of his crisp, black curls shining against a background of leaves and blue sky, his eyes a deeper blue contrasting with the tan of his well-formed features, would stay with her for the rest of her life.

Is it not enough that I love you for your innate goodness and kindness? she thought. *Do you also have to be the most handsome man I have ever encountered?* Suddenly she became aware that Marcus had resumed speaking.

"I beg your pardon," she said. "My mind wandered. Do you mind repeating that?"

"I should have realized. You had a faraway look in your eyes. I was asking you if you still came to the house to sew for my mother."

"Yes. As a matter of fact, she is entrusting me to embroider the bodice of a new ball gown for her."

"Splendid. I shall make a point of dropping by the sewing room for a chat from time to time."

An act of mercy? How terribly humiliating.

"That is very good of you, to be sure," she replied. "Now, if you please, I should like to go home before my mother finishes her nap."

"As you wish. Allow me to go first so that I may assist your descent."

Clarissa smiled in spite of the wretchedness she felt. "You always used to insist on climbing down first. Have you any idea how angry that used to make me?"

He grinned. "You used to pout and scowl until you realized it availed you nothing. I hope you are not planning on trying that now."

She shook her head. "After you. I have a feeling that Marcus the man is every bit as implacable as Marcus the boy. Besides, it would be most unpleasant if you were to miss your footing and land on me."

In one of those little ironies of life, upon reaching down from the lowest branch to grasp the hand Marcus so gallantly offered, Clarissa was the one who slipped and fell. With the fast reflexes of an athlete, Marcus opened his arms and caught her.

Still holding her in his arms, he staggered back a few steps before regaining his balance. To Clarissa's consternation, being held by Marcus had a greater impact than the actual fall. The subtle male scent of his body mingling with that of finely milled soap released a floodgate of emotion.

She felt the heat of embarrassment on her cheeks. Not knowing what else to do, she pushed firmly against his shoulders, saying, "Put me down. I am perfectly all right, thank you."

Marcus did so, looking obviously uncomfortable over the whole situation. An awkward silence ensued and then he said, "Are you sure? That was quite a drop."

"Perfectly sure. And you?"

"What about me?"

"You are not hurt?"

"Not in the least."

Clarissa forced a smile. "In that case, I shall bid you good-bye."

She went to drop him a curtsy. Discovering her skirt was still tucked in at the waist, she quickly tugged it free.

"I must say, Clarissa, you blush deeper and more often than any other young lady I know."

Clarissa sighed. "I suspect that is because I have more reason to do so. What must you think of me?"

"Granted, you do things that would not occur to other girls, but I accept the blame for that. It is unfortunate that you placed your trust in me."

"Unfortunate? I do not understand."

"I hate to say this, Clarissa," he said. "But unless you are more circumspect, some men will presume they have carte blanche to rob you of your virtue."

Clarissa fought the urge to slap his face. "You must take me for a fool."

"No, Clarissa, you are not a fool. It is your innocence that makes me fear for you."

"Arrgh!" Clarissa clenched her fists and stamped her foot. "They are one and the same. I have just one thing to say to you, Marcus Ridley."

"And that would be?"

"Good-bye!"

Marcus looked rueful. "My apologies, Clarissa. I did not mean to ruffle your feathers." Having said this, he bent down and kissed her on the forehead.

"Good-bye, old friend—for now."

His apology would have set better with Clarissa had she not noticed that he had the devil's own time trying not to laugh.

Chapter 11

Clarissa stared out of the living room window, an open book lying neglected on her lap. *The leaves on the trees are beginning to turn*, she thought. *Summer is over. Although it makes no difference to me.* The book slid out of her lap to land with a thud on the parquet floor.

Clarissa shot a furtive glance toward the hearth, where her mother sat knitting a scarf, praying that she had not heard it fall. But, alas, this was too much to hope for. Mrs. Carter looked askance over her small wire-rimmed glasses, first at the book and then Clarissa.

"Really, child. Be more careful, I beg of you. Should you damage that book, I would have no idea what to say to Lady Fairfax."

Clarissa retrieved the leather-bound book of poetry from the floor, relieved to find that it was none the worse for the fall. "I am truly sorry, Mama. I am afraid I was woolgathering."

"Your time would be far better spent if you finished sewing the trim on your dress. The Fairfax ball is only two days from now."

"I finished it yesterday, Mama."

"Then why have you not put it on for your Papa and me to see?"

Clarissa sighed. "Because I am not keen on the idea of attending the ball. Perhaps you and Papa can go without me."

Mrs. Carter put down her knitting. "Go without you? And risk incurring her ladyship's displeasure? It is out of the question."

"I am sure her ladyship will not mind."

"Then you are a fool, Clarissa. Lady Fairfax would not have

made you the gift of the beautiful ivory silk had she not wished you to attend."

Mrs. Carter pulled a kerchief from her reticule and dabbed her eyes. "What have I done to deserve such a difficult child? Heaven knows I have always put your needs before my own."

Clarissa stood up and, still clutching the book, hastened to her mother's side. "Please do not cry, Mama. Of course I shall go."

Her mother presented her cheek to Clarissa for a conciliatory kiss. "That is much better. You have been acting so strangely of late. I wonder if you are coming down with something."

Clarissa straightened up. "Do not fuss, Mama. I feel quite all right."

Her mother knitted her brow. "I am not so sure. You look so pale."

"That is because you make me wash my face in buttermilk and lemon juice to get rid of the freckles."

"Even so, I think you should get out in the fresh air more often. You hardly set foot over the sill these days. In fact, starting right now, I insist you resume your afternoon walks."

"But, Mama—"

"Not another word. Away with you, and do not forget to wear your bonnet. I should hate it if all the care we have given your skin came to naught."

"I left my bonnet upstairs, Mama."

"Then for goodness sake go and get it. I will not have you looking like a peasant."

Clarissa came downstairs a few minutes later, her bonnet tied firmly under her chin.

"You certainly took your time. Now get along with you."

Clarissa was halfway down the garden path when Mrs. Carter came running after her, holding a dark green cloak aloft.

"You forgot your cloak. I swear, child, it is a keeper you need."

"It is too warm for a cloak."

"*Take* it. You would argue with the angels."

Clarissa complied, but took it off when reaching the stile

and tossed it into the meadow. She hesitated for a moment, then lifted her skirts and attempted to vault the stile as Marcus had while escaping the bull. She acquired a bruised knee for her trouble.

Railing against her own stupidity, she picked up the cloak. Rather than go by the elm tree, a bitter reminder of the disastrous day she had spent with Marcus, she went west to the trout stream and followed it all the way to the farm.

On reaching the wall separating the piggery from the rest of the farm, she encountered Horace returning home, carrying a sack of potatoes Mrs. Gates had requested.

"Hello, Horace," she said. "Anything interesting to report?"

"I would say so," said Horace, his face fast turning red with excitement. "The whole farm is in an uproar."

"For goodness sake, tell me about it."

"Mr. Finch left this morning without so much as a fare-thee-well."

"Left? What do you mean?"

"Exactly what I said, Miss Clarissa. He packed up his worldly goods and hopped it. It seems that an uncle of his in America died and left him one of them cotton plantations. Did not give Lord Fairfax a minute's notice. Pure spite on his part."

"His lordship must be greatly inconvenienced."

"In more ways than one. It seems that Mr. Finch knew he was leaving for some time and deliberately neglected some of his duties. To top it off, this morning just before he left he let the livestock loose to roam all over the place."

"I *say*. Mr. Finch is sure to be held accountable for that."

"He'll be on the high seas before they can catch him."

Their conversation was interrupted by a grunting noise coming from behind the stone wall.

"What on earth can that be?" Clarissa asked.

"Sounds like a pig to me. A very contented pig, I should think."

Horace peered over the wall. "Yes, it's a pig. A large sow. She's having a good old time wallowing away in a huge mud hole."

Clarissa hastened to see for herself. "Who would put a pig wallow against a stone wall? By the look of it, the water for the mud is channeled from the duck pond in the adjoining field. It is only a matter of time before the wall tumbles down."

"Mr. Finch, without a doubt," Horace replied.

"How perverse," Clarissa added. "I wonder why he would take the trouble to do such a thing."

"To get back at the young master? That business about the smelly pig wallow must've riled Mr. Finch no end."

"What a dreadful man."

Horace shrugged. "It could be worse. He could've set fire to the hay barn or poisoned the livestock."

Clarissa shuddered. "Thank goodness he left."

Horace nodded. "I wager all the farm workers feel the same way. I hear he was a devil to work for."

The church bell chimed the quarter hour.

"I had better be off," he said. "Mrs. Gates will be looking for these potatoes. Are you coming?"

"Not yet. I think I'll stay and watch this sow for a while. She is very amusing."

Marcus strolled through the grounds of Fairfax Towers, basking in the warmth of the afternoon sun. It was such an unexpected pleasure so late in September, and in a buoyant mood, he determined to savor every minute.

However, when he reached the oak tree, this feeling was quenched by waves of nostalgia. He ran both hands across the rough bark of the ancient tree and, recalling happier times, mourned his lost childhood.

Life was less complicated then. He stepped back from the tree, debating whether or not to climb it for old time's sake, but decided against it. It would not be the same without a companion to share the experience, and John was married.

Clarissa came to mind. *Perish the thought*. Without thinking, he flexed his right hand and winced. His wrist still hurt from the sprain he had sustained when breaking her fall from the elm the month before.

Bertie is right. If I value my life, I should keep my distance from that hot-tempered brat.

His reverie was broken by the sound of a girlish voice calling out his name. He looked up to see a fair-haired young female dressed in pink muslin hurrying across the lawn toward him.

"Oh no!" he groaned. "It's that inane little chatterbox, Samantha Nelson, and what is worse, she has that look about her. I refuse to be stalked by yet another juvenile huntress. They are so lacking in finesse. Makes it impossible for a chap to back out of a situation with any grace."

Marcus continued his stroll, carefully maintaining a leisurely pace while in her line of vision. On rounding a clump of shrubbery, the path became a tree-lined lane leading directly to the farm.

Samantha is a small girl. Runs like a duck, actually. I am bound to reach the farm before she turns the corner. Then all I have to do is vault the wall.

Marcus quickened his pace and made all speed. Directly ahead was the small bridge which spanned the trout stream and, beyond that, sanctuary in the form of the old stone wall.

He did not notice Clarissa perched atop the high wall until he was halfway across the bridge. He wondered how she had managed to shimmy up there trammeled by all that muslin. He saw her hastily pull at her skirts, but not before he caught sight of the infamous breeches.

Good lord, the girl is absolutely incorrigible, he thought.

Without stopping to exchange pleasantries he yelled, "Go home, Clarissa, and get rid of those damned breeches before they get you in trouble."

She looked at him in open-mouthed surprise and yelled, "Stop!"

Too late. By then he was soaring over the wall in a graceful arc. The next thing he knew he was floundering in mud next to a huge sow that proceeded to shatter his eardrums with an ever-growing crescendo of indignant squeals.

To add to his outrage, he espied Clarissa looking down at

him, vainly trying to smother a laugh. "I am glad you find it amusing," he roared. "Why in thunder did you not warn me?"

"I did. If you had not been so busy pontificating, you would have heard."

"You impudent little chit," he spluttered. "You should be—be—" Too angry to think straight, he clamped his mouth shut. Besides, with the sow thrashing about, he was in danger of getting mud in it.

"I do apologize, but you must admit that it is awfully funny."

"I admit nothing of the sort, and I doubt you would either if our positions were reversed."

"Perhaps not." Clarissa removed her bonnet and cast it to the ground. "Would not do to soil it," she explained, extending her hand to him. "Let me help you out of there. You are upsetting that poor pig no end."

"I am upsetting the *pig?* For your information, the vile creature just kicked my leg with one of her trotters. Those things are as sharp as knives."

"I have heard that such is the case," Clarissa replied gravely. "You should let me help you out of there before she takes it into her head to finish you off."

"Finish me *off?* Why, you wretched girl, I do believe you are enjoying my predicament. Stop waving your hand at me. I can manage without your help, thank you very much."

He struggled to a standing position and made a tentative step toward the edge of the wallow. To his chagrin, he lost his footing and landed on his back.

Apparently disgusted with the intruder invading her territory, the sow delivered Marcus a glancing blow to his other leg and scrambled out of the wallow.

"Ouch!" Marcus yowled, manfully refraining from uttering the profanities that would have tripped so readily from his lips had Clarissa not been present. "Why is it that this mud presents no problem to that mountain of lard, yet I cannot take one step without falling over?"

The question was rhetorical, but Clarissa answered it anyway. "Evidently kicking is not the only advantage trotters give to pigs," she replied.

She offered him her hand once more. He hesitated for a moment, and then, swallowing his pride, grasped it and began inching closer to the wall. As he reached to grab the top with his free hand, he lost his footing and fell back into the mud.

Unfortunately, he failed to let go of Clarissa's hand. With a piercing shriek, she joined him in the pig wallow, her left foot, encased in a sturdy brown shoe, hitting him squarely in the right eye.

Why not? he reasoned, wincing with pain. *Clearly, this girl was put on this earth to torment me.*

Strangely enough, coming to this conclusion seemed to lift a weight off his shoulders. All he had to do was give her a wide berth. How difficult could that be?

Next to impossible. What are the chances of finding Clarissa Carter lying in wait like some avenging angel of death the one time I find it necessary to vault over a wall? Probably the same as landing in a pig wallow that was nonexistent two days prior, he thought gloomily. *It is no use worrying about it. If I were to dash off to Timbuktu, it is a foregone conclusion that she would be waiting for me, no doubt with a horde of hungry cannibals in tow.*

To his horror she pushed her mud-caked face close to his. "Are you all right? I know my foot made contact with some part of your anatomy." She looked mortified. "Oh, Marcus, your poor eye. I am dreadfully sorry."

She lifted her hand as if to pat his face and he fended her off. "Spare me your sympathy, Clarissa. It is apt to kill me."

Clarissa drew back. "Yes, I suppose you would think that. Th-things just seem to *happen* when we are together."

Even through the heavy layer of mud caking her face, Marcus could see that she was on the verge of crying. He had not seen Clarissa cry since she was a very little girl and did not relish seeing her do so now.

He gave her a reassuring pat, mud dripping from his hand. "Steady on there. It is not your fault. As you so aptly put it, things happen when we are together, and I for one have not the foggiest notion why. They just *do.*"

Clarissa regarded him, her large eyes shimmering like aquamarines behind a veil of unshed tears.

She is not the prettiest girl I have ever met. Does not even come close. Of course, all that mud does not help matters—but those eyes. Not even Celeste's can compare.

"And now your eye has turned red and is beginning to swell," Clarissa replied, intruding on his thoughts. "What possessed you to jump over the wall in the first place? You came haring down the lane as if the devil were chasing you."

"An apt description. I was trying to get away from a garrulous young houseguest. She showed every sign of being another Primrose, and to be frank, I was not in the mood to cope with her."

"Unless she is coming after you on her hands and knees, I think it is safe to say she gave up the chase. There was no one following you."

Marcus felt foolish. "I could have saved us both a lot of trouble."

As he spoke, Clarissa struggled to her feet. "If you help me, perhaps I can make it to the bank. I am closer to it than you. The sooner we get out of here, the better. That sow is liable to return with other members of her family. Clyde the boar comes to mind."

"In that case…" Marcus got on his knees and, putting his hand on the small of her back, propelled her to the edge of the bank.

Clarissa staggered two steps before losing her balance, then plopped face down in the mud. She was struggling to get up when Marcus called out, "No. Stay where you are. There is a huge tuft of grass directly in front of you. Use it to pull yourself up."

Blinded by the mud, Clarissa did as he asked and after much fumbling, grasped the tuft. She hung on to it while securing a foothold and then hauling herself out of the mud. She used the grass to wipe her face, then turned to glare at Marcus, her fists clenched in fury. "You pushed me!"

"I did not mean to. I was trying to facilitate your escape and evidently applied more pressure than was called for. Now, if you will be so kind, you can use that broken tree branch over there to help pull me out."

Clarissa stood by the edge of the wallow with both hands on her hips and glowered at him. "Find your own way out of there, for I will not raise a finger to help you."

"How do you propose I do that?"

"The same way I did. Stand up, take a couple of steps, and then fall on your face. I am sorry I am not there to give you a push, but I think you can manage."

Marcus could not credit what he was hearing. This impudent chit who was not his equal either in age or rank had the temerity to give him a thorough set-down? He was in the process of getting all puffed up with a sense of his own importance when he was hit with a strong dose of reality.

At that moment in time, he was merely a man sitting up to his armpits in mud and looking extremely foolish in the process. Getting out of it was up to him, so the sooner he got on with it, the better. Even so, he could not let the matter rest.

"Very well, Clarissa. I am sure I shall manage well enough without you."

"I am sure you shall," she replied, a look of complete indifference on her face.

"You disappoint me. This is a side of you I have not seen before. I had no idea you could be so vindictive. It must be the ginger hair."

Clarissa looked grim. "I think you will be in a better position to judge after you have had mud clogging every orifice of your head."

Touché.

"I understand. Because of me, you have suffered an ordeal that would cause most young ladies to take to their beds until Christmas. Then, instead of apologizing, I cast aspersions on your character and compounded the insult with disparaging remarks regarding the color of your hair. I hope you can forgive me."

Clarissa did not answer.

Evidently not. It is no more than I deserve. Perhaps it is for the better.

It is time we both put this odd friendship behind us.

Shrugging, Marcus started to get up. To his surprise, Clarissa held her hand up. "Do not move," she called. "At least, not until I get the tree branch."

He watched her go for the branch with an appreciative eye for her easy, loose-limbed stride.

I'll say this for Clarissa, she is as graceful as a gazelle. Not a hint of a mince or a trace of a waddle in her walk, and I'll wager she comes by it naturally. No balancing of books on the head for that one.

Once Marcus was clear of the wallow, they regarded one another with dismay.

"We make a sorry sight, I must say," Marcus said.

Clarissa looked down at her dress. "What am I going to do? My parents will be absolutely livid about this. Of a certainty I shall not be allowed to attend your ball."

"Do not worry about it. I shall see to it that you are exonerated. By the time I have finished, everyone will consider you a heroine."

"Do you think so?"

"Absolutely. Right up there with Boudicca and Joan of Arc, I should imagine. In the meantime, a dip in the stream is in order. It should get the worst of this mud off."

They eschewed climbing the wall in favor of using a gate situated about twenty yards north. On reaching the stream, Clarissa slipped her shoes off and wrinkled her nose at the thick clumps of mud and grass adhering to them. While waiting for Marcus to pull his boots off, she edged her way down to the stream bed.

"Hold on, there, Clarissa. Before you take another step, take off those breeches. Mrs. Cole will have a fit if she catches you wearing those."

Clarissa's face flamed. "Here? In front of you?"

Marcus laughed. "I promise not to look. Besides, you may relax safely in the knowledge that I find nothing provocative about a girl wearing a pair of my muddy breeches."

"That was not my concern," Clarissa replied, clearly irked by his words. "I merely question the propriety of such a thing."

That could have been worded better, I suppose—and to think they call John the tactless one of the family.

"It is a little late to question the propriety of this afternoon's doings. Take them off behind those bushes at the water's edge, if it will make you feel any better, and let me know when it is all right for me to join you. In the meantime, I shall be scraping the mud off our footwear."

Presently, Clarissa emerged from behind the bushes and waded toward the center of the stream until the water came up to her waist. The mud leached from her clothes, dissolving in the water and streaking downstream in swirling brown ribbons.

Marcus waded out to join her. "You could have told me the water was cold."

"It would have served no purpose."

"I suppose not. Well, here goes." He took a deep breath and submerged his head. The water stung his injured eye. Not wishing to linger, he quickly ran his fingers through his hair and behind his ears to get rid of the mud and quickly emerged in a spray of water.

Clarissa's forehead knitted in concern. "You should have that eye attended to as quickly as possible. It is turning purple."

"The sooner you get the mud out of your hair, the sooner we can leave."

Clarissa ran her fingers through her hair and removed a sodden ribbon and what pins the mud had not claimed. Marcus took them from her.

"Good. Now duck under and give your hair a thorough going over with your fingers."

Clarissa hesitated for a moment. Then, with a look of grim resolve, she inhaled and plunged her head into the water. When she emerged, Marcus gave her an assessing look.

"That will do," he said. "Now if you will give me your hand, we shall get out of here and be on our way."

Chapter 12

Mrs. Carter watched young Viscount Ridley's dark gray curricle round the bend of the lane with the satisfaction of a tabby that has managed to knock over a pail of cream. Once the stylish vehicle was out of sight she turned from the window beaming with pleasure.

"Fancy that. His lordship brought you home in his new curricle. To my way of thinking, it was only proper. That business of sending you home in the servant's wagon never sat well with me."

To Clarissa's surprise, her mother came over to the hearth and actually hugged her, then stepped back and fingered the violet-colored kerseymere coat Clarissa had on.

"It is hardly worn. Are you sure her ladyship said you could keep it?"

"Yes, Mama. She made it very plain that I could keep everything. I suppose that since my own clothes were ruined helping Lord Ridley out of the pig wallow, she thought it the appropriate thing to do."

"But she gave you her finest clothes. These are not castoffs." Mrs. Carter crossed her arms over her shoulders and with an excited little giggle gave herself a hug. "Something wonderful will come of this, you will see. I hope you realize how fortunate you are to enjoy the gracious condescension of such a high-in-the-in-step lady."

Mr. Carter, who had been quietly reading his newspaper, stood up, his body stiff with outrage. "And *I*, madam, say that *nothing* good can possibly come from this. Good lord, that young scamp brings our daughter home with some taradiddle about her rescuing him from a pig wallow? Come now. The man is big ough to take care of himself."

"But it is true, Papa. Every word. You saw how awful his eye looks."

"Surely, Edwin, her ladyship would not have received Clarissa so kindly if there were the slightest chance that something untoward had taken place."

Mr. Carter looked skeptical. "You think not? Lady Fairfax has always dealt fairly with us, but she is an aristocrat. I am sure she would do everything in her power to gloss over a scandal rather than risk having someone like our Clarissa for a daughter-in-law."

"Papa! That is a perfectly horrid thing to say."

"That will be enough, Clarissa." He turned to his wife. "A lot of this can be laid at your door, madam. Our daughter roams around the countryside like a gypsy, and when she lands in a pickle all you do is rhapsodize over the good it may do her. What good could come of this?"

"Papa!"

"Go to your chamber, girl. I will see to you later. This is between your mother and me."

Clarissa was devastated. Until now, her father had never raised his voice to her. As she sat in her room listening to the heated exchange of words between her parents, she recalled the admonishment she had received from Mrs. Cole while waiting below stairs at Fairfax Towers for her bathwater to heat.

"Mind how you go where the young master is concerned. You are not like some of the females that cavort around here. I swear, the higher their instep, the lower their morals."

"There is nothing between Lord Ridley and me. It was purely by chance that we met this afternoon."

"That is all well and good, Clarissa, but stay away. Too many of these chance meetings could result in trouble for you. You would not be the first innocent to be robbed of her virtue by the honeyed words of a handsome young lord."

Clarissa's face flamed with embarrassment as she recalled the well-meaning housekeeper's words. "It is not like that at all," she murmured as she sat in her darkening chamber. "Why, oh why do older people look for evil where there is none? It is well that Marcus and I have no intention of seeking each other's company again. After such a terrible insinuation, I would be too embarrassed to face him." She let out a groan. "Oh no. How could I have forgotten? The ball at Fairfax Towers is to take place the day after tomorrow. Perhaps Papa will forbid me to attend."

Even as she uttered the words, Clarissa did not wish them to be true, for Marcus had promised to dance with her.

"I say, Marcus," Bertie said. "For a country ball, this is quite a crush. Where did your mother find all these people?"

"In the neighboring shires, I should imagine. Invitations to Fairfax are seldom turned down."

"Where is this Clarissa person? If I have to dance with her, I might as well get it over with. Although I must admit, old chap, that patch on your eye makes the thought of getting close to her a little frightening."

"You have nothing to worry about. I seem to be the only one who has reason to fear her."

"Most peculiar. One could call her your nemesis."

"Come now, Bertie, there is no need for dramatics. She is standing under the musician's gallery. The tall girl wearing orange spencer."

"Ah yes. She must rival your mother in stature, and what glorious titian hair she has."

"Titian? It looks ginger to me."

"Then you must be blind. And by the way, her jacket is more apricot than orange. Goes deucedly well with her coloring."

As Bertie skirted around the green and gold ballroom to request a dance, Marcus noticed there was not a trace of a limp to his gait. He had been right. A couple of months at Bath had done Bertie a world of good.

He looked at Clarissa once more. *Glorious titian hair? It must be the candlelight. By Jove, that spencer looks a trifle snug. When did she acquire that bosom, I wonder?*

"Yes, she is striking, is she not?"

Marcus turned to see Celeste Markham looking up at him, an amused smile on her face.

"I have never known you to be taken with redheads before," she added.

Confound you, Celeste.

Marcus put on his most charming smile and bowed to her. "Alas, *cherie*, the only redhead who can lay claim to my heart is you, and you have no use for it whatsoever."

Celeste tapped him with her fan. "Such a charming liar. I rather suspect that your honeyed words gave cause for the black patch you have over your eye. Have a care, darling, lest a jealous husband cut you down in your prime. Who is she?"

"Who?"

"The girl with the titian hair, of course."

"Why, all of a sudden, is everyone using the term titian for perfectly ordinary ginger hair? She is Clarissa Carter, the daughter of my father's steward."

"Ah! Say no more."

"What do you mean by that?"

"Nothing. Only according to John's reports regarding your dealings with her, Miss Carter *has* to be responsible for that dreadful black eye you are sporting."

"Then I think John is in need of a set-down. He is very careless with other people's confidences."

"You will have to wait. He just asked Miss Carter to dance the cotillion. Your friend Bertie should have moved a little faster."

"Celeste, if you will just keep quiet for a moment, I shall ask you to dance with me."

She cocked her head to one side. "What lady could resist such a charming offer?"

"Splendid. I see Lancelot Thurgood and his partner are seeking another couple."

"Lancelot Thurgood? And who might he be?"

"Just a neighbor. A widower Mother thinks might be a match for Clarissa."

Celeste shook her head. "Your mother is making a terrible mistake. The gentleman looks old enough to be the girl's father."

Marcus saw the concern in her eyes. Celeste was qualified to voice an opinion on the matter. She had been prevailed upon to enter a marriage of convenience at the tender age of sixteen to a man old enough to be her grandfather. Contrary to the gossip mills, he suspected that Celeste had never experienced the joys of passionate love.

"My sentiments exactly, but my mother is inordinately fond of Clarissa and wishes to secure a comfortable life for her," he replied as they made their way across the ballroom floor.

Lancelot Thurgood introduced his partner, a fading beauty of an uncertain age, as his cousin Elsie. She had, he explained, come to run his household and to help him raise his six motherless children.

Marcus surmised that Miss Thurgood had made her debut at least a decade before the turn of the century and had received no offers of marriage. At least, none she had been allowed to accept.

When Marcus suggested that they should join forces and make up the foursome required to dance the cotillion, Miss Thurgood indulged in an inane fit of the giggles, accompanied by several coy pats to the graying curls perched atop her head. However, when the orchestra struck up a lively tune, she proved to be a very skilful dancer, giving Marcus cause to believe that the lady had been popular in her heyday.

On leaving the dance floor, Celeste said, "You failed to mention that Mr. Thurgood has six children. For pity's sake, Marcus, at least one or two of them have to be older than your Clarissa. You must do all in your power to see that nothing comes of your mother's plans."

"Clarissa has a mind of her own. I doubt she would marry where her heart does not lie. In fact, I get the impression that she is not in the least bit interested in marrying anyone."

Celeste arched her brow. "Really? So the subject of matrimony has arisen? I find that *most* interesting."

"Stop it, Celeste. You are being tiresome. Of course I have

not entered into such a discussion with the girl. She is far too young for me, besides which, I do not find her attractive in the least."

"Then you are one of the few gentlemen in the room who does not. She has not lacked for a dance partner since she entered the room. Even the shorter gentlemen seem not to be put off by her stature."

To Marcus's relief, a Mr. Aubrey Sinclair, a distinguished looking gentleman in his middle forties, approached to claim Celeste. Gossip had it that since the required mourning period for his deceased wife was over, the handsome, very rich widower was seeking another bride.

He would be perfect for Celeste, Marcus thought as he watched them line up for the next dance. He suddenly remembered that he had promised the dance to one of several young ladies his mother had invited for the weekend. In fact, his mother had seen to it that he was obligated for the three dances following, each with a different girl.

As he made his way to where his would-be partner sat impatiently tapping her foot, out of the corner of his eye he saw Bertie escorting Clarissa over to a cluster of young couples forming a square for the quadrille.

Bertie, you are fawning over her like a damned fool. Look at you, wearing her on your arm like a battle trophy. You and I are due for a talk, my fine fellow. I will not have you treat Clarissa as though she were a tavern wench.

His chance to talk to Bertie came right after fulfilling his obligation to dance with the fourth young lady on his mother's list. He had not warmed to any of his dance partners and, feeling somewhat jaded over the matter, stepped out onto the balcony to get some fresh air.

Leaning on the balustrade, he gazed absently at the moon rising over the treetops and pondered the matter. Of the four, he had found his last partner, a Miss Annette Palmer, to be the most tolerable, but then she was considerably older than the trio of giggling Bath misses who had preceded her.

I wonder if Mother arranged that on purpose. The Palmer girl is pretty in a quiet sort of way, but she does not stir my blood. What am I supposed to do? Continue with one meaningless affair after another, or settle for marriage to a girl whom I find merely tolerable? That is not the sort of life I had envisioned.

His reverie was broken by the weight of a hand placed on his shoulder. He turned and saw it was Bertie, a broad smile on his face.

"Thought it was you I saw coming out here." Bertie stretched out his arms and took a deep breath. "Aah! The night air feels good."

He took his place beside Marcus and leaned on the balustrade. "How are you coming along with the fillies your mother lined up for you? Any of them take?"

"No, they did not. The Palmer girl was all right, I suppose, but is that what it comes down to?"

"Eh? I do not follow."

"Do most men choose wives for their suitability rather than love?"

"Damned silly question, if you ask me. You know full well that most marriages among the *ton* are contracted to conserve fortunes, not to consummate love. That is probably why as soon as an heir has been produced, so many married couples scurry about like rabbits taking one lover after another."

"I would rather see John's line inherit the earldom than settle for that. This brings me to another thing, I saw how you carried on with Clarissa."

"*Carried* on? What on earth are you talking about?"

"With all that wit and charm, you had her positively eating out of your hand. Stay away from her. I will not have you ruining her life."

"Steady on. If we were not old friends, I would have popped your cork by now. I have no designs on your precious Clarissa. I was merely trying to amuse her. When she smiles, this fascinating little dimple quirks the left side of her mouth."

"The right."

"Eh?"

"The right. It is definitely on the right. Like a crescent moon."

Bertie grinned. "So you have noticed? And by the way, if I were taken with the girl, I would do the honorable thing and pay her court. It hurts me to think that you would presume otherwise. After all, my expectations are such that I do not have to choose a wife based on her rank and the size of her dowry."

"How would your parents react to such an arrangement?"

"With their blessings, I would hope. After all, as with your parents, theirs was a love match."

Feeling thoroughly chastised, Marcus managed a rueful smile. "I made a thorough cake of myself, did I not?"

"One could say so. But under the circumstances it is not surprising."

"What are you implying?"

"Nothing. Nothing at all. For goodness sake, Marcus, there is no need to get your hackles up. I merely meant that you have known Clarissa since she was a little poppet. It is only natural for you to be protective of her. If some bounder were to trifle with my little sister, I would strangle them with my bare hands."

"Quite. I suppose I had better go inside. The dance I promised to Clarissa will be starting in a few minutes. Not that she is lacking for partners. I wonder why she is so popular."

"In case you have not noticed, Clarissa Carter is a very beautiful girl."

"Come now. Clarissa's looks are passable, but one can hardly call her pretty."

"I did not say she is pretty."

"I am afraid you have lost me."

Bertie looked askance. "I am not surprised. You are completely lacking in the discernment required to really appreciate women. This probably comes of never having to pursue any of them."

"I am sure you are about to enlighten me."

"Take the landscapes that my sister Arabella paints. Very pretty, are they not?"

"Arabella is a fine watercolorist."

"But I doubt you remember what any of them look like."

"Where is this leading?"

"The difference between pretty pictures and fine art can be applied to women. Even in this, Arabella can be used as an example."

"But Arabella's features are perfect."

"Exactly. Not a thing one could or *would* do to change their symmetry, is there?"

"Of course not."

"Describe Clarissa for me."

"Clarissa *does* have beautiful eyes. They are large and clear and the most extraordinary color. Oh yes, and her neck is long and gracefully arched." Marcus shrugged. "Other than that…"

"Come, man, you are not even trying. What about her mouth?"

"Far too wide."

"But do you not love the way that it curves up, as if she is enjoying a deliciously wicked little secret? And that smile!"

"What about it?"

"Come now, I'll bet even you go out of your way to make her smile."

"What if I do?"

"There you are, and we have yet to mention her magnificent bosom."

"I did not even notice she had one until this evening— see here, Bertie, this conversation has gone far enough. We are discussing a respectable girl, not a demimondaine."

"A girl, you will allow, with a most fascinating visage. One, I should imagine, that would captivate the right man for the rest of his life."

"Are you sure you are feeling all right? No fever or anything? You are raving like a bloody lunatic."

Bertie shrugged. "If it pleases you to think so. In the meantime, I suggest you hurry. You do not want to keep a lady waiting."

Marcus entered the ballroom, muttering, "Balderdash. Absolute balderdash. Bertie is going to end up locked in the family attic if he is not careful."

A quick sweep of the room proved Clarissa to be standing

in a corner conversing with John and Althea. Clarissa was taller than John by a good two inches and Althea by eight, so she was not difficult to spot.

As he walked over to them, Althea turned and waved. This made him smile. He remembered the time when his beautiful little sister-in-law would have died rather than draw attention to herself.

"It is about time you came to claim your partner," she said, once he had joined them. "Miss Carter has had to refuse two perfectly nice young gentlemen while waiting for you."

"I am not surprised," Marcus said gallantly. "Bertie is right. Apricot becomes you very well, Miss Carter."

Clarissa glowed with pleasure at the compliment.

She does look well this evening. Even her freckles are not so noticeable.

After an exchange of bows and curtsies, Marcus ushered Clarissa toward Celeste and her partner, who proved to be none other than Aubrey Sinclair. *They have evidently hit it off*, Marcus thought. *Let us hope that it takes.*

After the dance, Celeste suggested that the four of them should retire to the next room to partake of refreshments.

"I should like to become better acquainted with Miss Carter," she said. "After all, we are the only two ladies in the room who have ginger hair."

"Titian hair, my dear Lady Camberly," Aubrey Sinclair offered. "It is far too rich a shade to be called ginger."

This earned Mr. Sinclair a flirtatious look from Celeste.

"La, sir, it is very gallant of you to say so, do you not agree, Miss Carter?"

"Very gallant," Clarissa echoed.

Marcus suppressed a smile. *Tread softly, Celeste, darling*, he thought silently. *He is definitely nibbling but do not jerk the line until he is well and truly hooked.*

Aubrey Sinclair entwined his arm through Celeste's, saying, "After you, Lord Ridley. I know from experience that Fairfax balls always include a most delicious array of food."

Marcus hesitated for a moment, knowing full well that if he escorted the steward's daughter into the other room rather one of the other young ladies attending the ball, it might lead his parents and hers to question the nature of their friendship.

"Nothing would give me greater pleasure than to partake of refreshments with Miss Carter, but I do not think her father would approve."

Clarissa wrinkled her nose. "It would give cause for tongues to wag, and my father is cross with me as it is. In any case, my parents will expect me to accompany them to the refreshment table presently."

"In that case, Miss Carter," Marcus said, offering her his arm, "I shall escort you to where they are sitting."

"How disappointing," Celeste said. "Perhaps another time, Miss Carter."

"It is very gracious of you to say so, your ladyship," Clarissa replied, dropping Celeste a curtsy.

"Most disappointing," Aubrey Sinclair inserted, without looking the least bit sorry. Then, as if as an afterthought, he added, "But of course, sir, you will no doubt join us after you have delivered Miss Carter to her parents?"

"Perhaps," Marcus replied. "But kindly proceed without me. One is apt to be waylaid while wending through a roomful of people."

Celeste smiled.

As Marcus escorted Clarissa to where her parents were seated, he noticed a remarkable change in her attitude. She had lost her glow. Her lips no longer curved in the enigmatic manner that had so intrigued Bertie, but were clamped shut.

Evidently she questioned his reasons for their not taking refreshments together. *But one would have never known by her response. Such a game girl. I will wager she had not committed to eat with her parents, either. She carried that off like a true thoroughbred.*

His suspicions were confirmed when he saw the questioning look in her parents' eyes on expressing the hope that he had delivered Clarissa to them in a timely fashion.

He took his leave of the Carters and sought the balcony once more. As he leaned on the balustrade, he noticed that the moon was now riding high in the sky. It occurred to him that it had taken the moon but a short while to rise so high.

And for me to hurt Clarissa's feelings, even less. I would like to undo the damage, but besides making me look like a conceited ass to refine on the matter, it would blow the incident way out of proportion.

With a sigh of resignation, Marcus turned and entered the ballroom. It was time for him to dance with yet another possible future bride.

Chapter 13

The Carters went home from the ball in the same manner in which they had arrived—in a carriage complete with a groom generously provided by their hosts, Mrs. Carter chattering like a magpie from doorstep to doorstep.

Once within the confines of their own parlor, Mr. Carter lit several candles from the fire Mrs. Gates had banked in anticipation of their return. The room took on an intimate glow.

"To think our Clarissa made such a brilliant splash," Mrs. Carter gushed. "Not the richest heiress present danced more than she." She clasped a hand to her bosom. "And with such eligibles. Mr. Thistlethwaite danced with her twice! Twice, mind you. Such a feather in her cap."

"And a feather is *all* she will get from such doings," her husband snapped.

"Mr. Carter, why must you spoil everything?"

He gave a long-suffering sigh and looked at Clarissa. "Go to bed, child. Your mother and I have to talk."

Clarissa picked up one of the candlesticks and quickly left the room. As she climbed the stairs she heard him say, "Sit down, Beatrice, and let's get this over with."

She heard the complaining creak of the sofa springs as her mother sat down.

"Beatrice, all this silliness has to stop."

"Is it silly to want the best for our daughter?"

"Wanting and getting are two very different things. You are like a child playing make-believe. A handsome prince is not about to ask for Clarissa's hand in marriage, and to encourage her to believe otherwise is cruel."

"But such things do happen on rare occasions."

115

"I have heard enough nonsense for one night. You have no right to raise her hopes concerning the young gentlemen who were kind enough to dance with her."

"But I could be right. There were so many! Surely one of them could have taken a fancy to her. There has been a remarkable improvement in her looks."

"Should that day arrive, I shall be only too happy to admit I was wrong."

"On your knees?"

"On my knees, Beatrice. But truth be told, Clarissa could be the prettiest girl in all of Surrey and not one of those young bucks would offer her his name. A discreet little town house close to the theaters, perhaps, but nothing more."

"Oh, Edwin, do you really think one of them would dare to suggest such a dreadful thing?"

"Not really. But neither do I think they will be queuing at our garden gate to pay her court. The three of us had a jolly time. Let it go at that."

"Yes, we did. I thought I looked rather well this evening."

Clarissa heard the distinctive sound her father's chair always made when he stood up, and then heard him walk across the parquet floor.

"You were the prettiest one in the room, Beatrice," he said. His tone was intimate. This was followed by what sounded suspiciously like a kiss.

The storm had blown over. It was comforting to know that in spite of their differences, her parents did have some affection for each other.

Doubting that her mother would be in to help her unfasten her dress, Clarissa placed the candlestick on the nightstand and struggled out of her clothes as best she could.

It was almost dawn when she crawled into bed. Her father had grumbled about the late hours the aristocracy kept long before the musicians played their last tune, and as Clarissa shivered between the icy sheets, she was inclined to agree. Of course, as he had pointed out, they did have a jolly time.

She had almost spoiled it by questioning Marcus's motives

in refusing to escort her to the refreshment table. But common sense prevailed. In all the years she had known him, Marcus had never lied to her. Ashamed for having doubted him, Clarissa had put the incident behind her.

It was as her father predicted. Not one of her dance partners came to call on her, but unlike her mother, Clarissa had not expected them to. Lord and Lady Fairfax's houseguests left three days later, and with them, Marcus.

October and November went by and Marcus did not return to Fairfax Towers. According to the society column in the newspaper, in October, Lord Ridley was numbered among the Prince Regent's dinner guests at Carlton House. And toward the end of November, he retreated to the warmer clime of Cornwall to enjoy the hospitality of that most august couple, Mr. and Mrs. Gordon Thistlethwaite.

With a pang, Clarissa remembered his visit to Bath and the stories connecting him with the beautiful Arabella Thistlethwaite.

Could it be that Marcus is visiting the Thistlethwaites for the express purpose of offering for their daughter? It would be considered a brilliant match.

Clarissa was still agonizing over this possibility on December fifth, the day she celebrated her eighteenth birthday. To mark the occasion, Mrs. Gates had baked a special fruitcake, laced with brandy and encased in marzipan and decorated with a hard white icing.

"My goodness, Mrs. Gates. It is absolutely delicious," Mrs. Carter enthused. "But more fitting for a wedding, I should think."

"Just practicing. The way Clarissa is blooming, it will not be long before the offers will be rolling in."

"Much good would it do, Mrs. Gates," Mrs. Carter replied, glowering at Clarissa. "She refused out of hand to even meet with Mr. Thurgood—never mind the advantages such a match could afford her family. And he with that huge manor house and all."

"Come now, Beatrice," Mr. Carter remonstrated. "That was Clarissa's choice to make. It was never my intention to sell our daughter to the highest bidder."

117

"But…"

"Not another word. Clarissa has yet to open her present."

"A present for me, Papa?"

Her father kissed her cheek. "Yes, my dear. It is not every day that a young lady celebrates her eighteenth birthday."

He handed her a small black box. Biting her lips in anticipation, she opened it to find a pair of dramatic looking jet eardrops.

She turned to her father, and held one of them up to her ear. "Are they not the most beautiful things you ever saw? Thank you so much."

"Edwin, what were you thinking? They are far too long for a young girl."

"Nonsense," he countered. "Not if she has a beautiful swan neck like Clarissa."

Clarissa put them on and pushed her head forward. "See, Mama? They look perfect."

Mrs. Carter studied Clarissa for a moment, and said, "Hmmm. I see what you mean. Not every young lady could carry them off."

"That is not all," Mr. Carter added and handed Clarissa another box. Inside she found a black velvet ribbon with a jet drop, which was a perfect match to the earrings. She stared at it in wide-eyed amazement. "They will go beautifully with so many things!" she exclaimed.

"That is what the jeweler said when he recommended them to me."

After the dinner table was cleared, Mr. Carter sat reading the newspaper in his usual chair by the fire. When he was finished with it, he handed it to Clarissa. Little did he dream that this was a gift she would cherish far more than the beautiful earrings and pendant he had given her earlier on.

The very last paragraph in the society column clearly stated that Miss Arabella Thistlethwaite had just returned to the bosom of her family after a lengthy stay at her maternal grandparents' country-seat in Wiltshire.

• • •

Right after her birthday, Clarissa received a message from Lady Fairfax requesting her presence at Fairfax Towers the next morning. On hearing that a carriage was going to come for Clarissa, Mr. Carter commented on her ladyship's thoughtfulness.

"Harrumph!" Mrs. Carter snorted. "It is the very least she can do in this cold weather. It is to be hoped that a warm brick and a fur-lined lap robe are also provided for Clarissa."

Mrs. Carter had not had anything positive to say for Lady Fairfax ever since the ball. It was as if Mrs. Carter held her responsible for the young gentlemen who had been in attendance and had not courted Clarissa.

Clarissa arrived at Fairfax Towers at eleven o'clock the following morning, as arranged, and was ushered into the sewing room. Lady Fairfax, who was seated at the window working on some needlepoint, rose to greet her.

"Good morning, Clarissa. I must say you are looking very well."

Clarissa curtsied and returned the compliment.

"I am glad you are here." Lady Fairfax remarked. "I was getting awfully bored with this wretched embroidery. Who cares if one more footstool is refurbished? Not I, to be sure."

"Did you wish me to finish it for you?"

"Good heavens, no. I would not waste your talents on such a paltry thing. I wish you to embroider a bodice on a dress I have a fancy to wear for Christmas. Do you think you could do it on time?"

"Perhaps. But if it amounts to much I shall most likely have to take it home with me, rather than go back and forth."

"Hmm." Lady Fairfax cocked her head to one side. "I have a better idea. If your mother offers no objection, I would far rather you stayed here while you did it. The road is quite icy and it would safer for you. Besides, you would be good company for me."

"I could ask her," Clarissa replied, not at all sure her mother would agree to such an arrangement.

119

"No," Lady Fairfax responded. "As long as you are willing to stay, I shall take it upon myself to write your mother a note asking for her permission."

"My lady, it is far too good of you. I can hardly see how my mother can refuse."

A mischievous gleam danced in Lady Fairfax's sapphire blue eyes. "That is what I thought. Now come over here and tell me what you think should be done with this bodice."

On receiving the request for Clarissa to move into Fairfax Towers, Mrs. Carter almost swooned with excitement. "This could be a wonderful opportunity for Clarissa," she declared to Mr. Carter.

He regarded her over his spectacles. "Oh? I fail to see how, unless she wishes to take up dressmaking for a living. I suppose she *could* open a little shop in the village."

"Oh, Edwin. Please do not tease. Marcus Ridley is *bound* to come home for the holidays."

"Pray do not bark up that tree again, Beatrice. You have heard Clarissa on the subject. As far as his lordship is concerned, she is just an annoyance left over from his childhood."

Mrs. Carter gave a dismissive wave. "I do not give a fig for his high-and-mighty lordship. But think. That charming Mr. Thistlethwaite might accompany him, and he danced with our Clarissa *twice*. A clear sign he was taken with her! And I understand his father is every bit as rich as the earl."

"This is good reason for you not to entertain any idea of there being a match in it for our daughter. Since she refuses to accept money for her services, all Clarissa is going to get out of this is perhaps a few yards of material and, if she is lucky, some more of Lady Fairfax's castoffs."

"Then she has your permission to stay there?" Mrs. Carter asked, her voice quivering with excitement.

Mr. Carter threw up his hands. "I suppose so. There will be no peace in this house if I say otherwise."

Chapter 14

It did not take long for Clarissa's presence at Fairfax Towers to be firmly woven into the warp and weft of Lady Fairfax's life. Most days, Lady Fairfax joined Clarissa in the sewing room, and while plying their needles they indulged in friendly conversation, Lady Fairfax often regaling Clarissa with stories about the more eccentric members of the *ton*.

"But I assure you, every word is true," she said one morning, when Clarissa doubted one of her stories. "Lord Petersham actually put his wife under lock and key. As it turned out, it was he who was mad, not poor Lady Petersham, but no one realized it.

"Then, during the May festival one year, the man ripped off his clothes and proceeded to chase the maidens all over the village green, declaring that as a satyr he was entitled to keep as many of them as he could catch."

Clarissa burst out laughing, stopping long enough to say, "Of course you are joking, your ladyship."

Lady Fairfax put her hand over her heart and said, "I swear."

Clarissa shook her head and laughed even louder.

"Truly. He has been locked up in the castle for the past ten years. At first, they put him in the north tower, but it proved to be far too chilly, so they moved him to the west tower to take advantage of the afternoon sun." Lady Fairfax started to giggle. "To this day, they still have difficulty persuading him to keep his clothes on."

They were still laughing when Marcus stuck his head around the door. "What could possibly be that funny?" he asked, and then spotted Clarissa. "Hello, Clarissa. Is my mother leading you astray?"

"I am not sure," Clarissa answered as soon as she could control her laughter. "Lady Fairfax just told me an incredible story about a Lord Petersham. Should I believe it?"

"Absolutely," he said. "Although I am not so sure it is quite the thing to be telling a young lady, are you, Mother?"

"If you are going to be pompous, Marcus, you may leave," Lady Fairfax replied. "In any case, when did you get here? You were not expected until next week."

"I only set foot over the threshold a moment ago, as you would have heard if you ladies had not been indulging in such raucous laughter."

"You are beginning to sound like a parson. I hope you do not intend to ruin Christmas for the rest of us."

Marcus smiled. "Just teasing." He turned to Clarissa. "By the way, I did not expect to see you here. Keeping well, I trust? Although there is no need to ask. You look to be in splendid health."

"It is kind of you say so."

"I think Clarissa looks absolutely marvelous," Lady Fairfax inserted. "I knew that once she stopped growing she would have no trouble putting on a little weight. I went through the same thing when I was a girl. I used to think that if one more spiteful girl called me daddy longlegs I would cheerfully murder her."

Clarissa's eyes widened. "But you are so beautiful, Lady Fairfax."

Lady Fairfax pinched her cheek. "What a darling child. Small wonder I like to have her about me."

"And why is Clarissa still sewing for you? Might one ask? I thought we agreed that you would not impose on her any further."

"It is no imposition. I like sewing for her ladyship. It is the only chance I get to work with such beautiful materials."

"I stand corrected," Marcus said. The longcase clock in the hallway struck three and he frowned. "It gets dark by four this time of year. Clarissa should be on her way home by now."

"If she were going home."

"Leading me to believe she is not?"

"My goodness Marcus, your grasp of the king's English is positively awe-inspiring. Clarissa will be with us for at least another week. There is no sense in her making that trip in the cold every day."

"A wise decision, to be sure. Now if you ladies will excuse me, I am going upstairs and getting into a hot bath as quickly as possible. We were beset by the north wind all the way from London, and I am chilled to the bone. I should not be the least bit surprised if it snowed tonight."

"He is a thoughtless scamp," Lady Fairfax remarked once he left the room. "This is the first time I have seen him since the ball, and not so much as a peck on the cheek did I receive from him."

"I think he was too shocked by our behavior to remember," Clarissa suggested. "Perhaps I should eat in the servants' hall tonight. I am sure you have a lot of family business to discuss."

"That is absurd. We have learned over the years not to air our grievances over the dinner table. It is bad for the digestion. Nothing will be discussed this evening that you cannot hear."

"How very wise." Clarissa forbore to add that such was not the case in the Carter household.

Lady Fairfax stood up. "I suggest we put away our sewing. We have been at it far too long."

Clarissa usually retreated to the library after she had finished sewing for the day—that is, if no one else was using it. This day she hurried to her chamber to see to her toilet.

Ordinarily she would have gone below stairs to procure a jug of hot water for the purpose, but knew that all the hot water would be earmarked for the young master's bath.

On reaching her room, she was grateful to see that the chambermaid had not let the fire die down. Even so, as with most country houses, a cold draft seeped through the window frames and under the door.

Gritting her teeth, she bathed in ice-cold water from the washstand bowl. *The facilities in this grand house are no better than the ones at ours*, she thought. *Except at home there is no chambermaid to supply the fresh water, or to see that the fire is kept burning.*

She dried off with a large linen towel she had warmed in front of the fire, and then, with her teeth chattering, put on a clean shift. Over that, she donned a cozy robe that Lady Fairfax had so thoughtfully supplied for her comfort.

As she huddled close to the fire, she caressed the soft, cream-colored wool covering her shoulders, murmuring, "I take it back. Nothing at our house feels as wonderful as this."

Basking in the warmth of the fire, she gradually relaxed and drifted off to sleep. She did not waken until Millie, the young chambermaid who had come in to light the oil lamp on her dressing table, bent over her to light a spill from the fire.

"Excuse me, miss. I did not see you lying there in the dark. Gave me quite a start."

Clarissa stretched her arms. "I must have nodded off. What time is it, please?"

"Almost six o' clock. Her ladyship said I should help you dress for dinner."

"That will not be necessary, Millie. My dress is not too difficult for me to fasten. Quite simple, really."

Millie lit the oil lamp, and as the flame was drawn into the glass chimney, the bedchamber flooded with a soft glow. "Her ladyship sent you one of her dresses. I laid it on your bed. You will not be getting into *that* without help."

Clarissa walked over to the bed and lifted the dress from the coverlet. It was made of a deep russet silk with an overlay of heavy ivory lace on the bodice. "It is beautiful. I wonder why she would want me to have it."

Millie cocked her head to one side. "Her ladyship has not worn it in the two years I've worked here. I doubt it fits her anymore."

"I have never worn anything so grand."

"Don't s'pose you have, miss, not being a countess. But I think you will do it proud."

"Why, thank you, Millie. How sweet of you to say so," Clarissa walked over to the dressing table and picked up her hairbrush, a fine, silver-backed piece Grandmother Carter had bequeathed to her.

"Sit down, miss. Let me do that for you," Millie said.

"That will not be necessary, Millie. You work hard enough as it is without having to wait on me."

"If you don't mind, I should like to. It is my dream to become a lady's maid one day, though there is not much chance of it happening."

"One never knows, Millie. Who would have thought I would be a guest in this house and allowed to dine with an earl and his lady every night?"

Millie took the hairbrush from Clarissa and shuddered. "I don't know how you do it, miss. I would be so nervous, I doubt I could get the food to stay on the fork long enough to reach my mouth."

Clarissa smiled. "The meals are not so elaborate at our house, but the same rules apply. My father did not come from a rich family, but they were comfortably situated."

"I remember my mum mentioning that," said Millie, vigorously applying the brush to Clarissa's hair. "Second son, wasn't he? And then, of course, you was packed off to Derbyshire to be educated with his brother's girls. Mum thought that was doing you a disservice at the time, but now I am not sure as I agree."

"I am glad I had the experience," Clarissa replied, wincing at the force Millie applied to the brush. "But as far as I can see, learning to do fine embroidery is the only advantage staying at my uncle's house afforded me. I would not be here if Lady Fairfax were not kind enough to admire my work."

"Everyone talks about that. I've heard said that her ladyship considers your work better than her fancy London mantua makers."

"My goodness," Clarissa rejoined. "I wonder where the villagers get their information."

"It was talked about in the servants' hall. Her ladyship makes no secret of the matter."

"I find that most distressing. The earl and his family have a right to their privacy."

"I doubt much goes on in this house that has to be hidden.

At least, not when the young lord stays away. The way some of those top-lofty ladies throw themselves at him is a disgrace. Hound the poor gentleman to death, they do."

Having no desire to dwell on the indignities Marcus Ridley suffered at the hands of would-be wives or lovers, Clarissa changed the subject. "I say, Millie. I never would have thought to arrange curls across my forehead. I hardly recognize my own face."

"I hope you like it, miss."

"I think so." Clarissa said, peering into the looking glass. "It is such a change. What are you going to do with the rest of it? It is so unruly."

"It is best to work with curls rather than fight them, so I am going to pin them atop your head and secure them with this." Millie handed Clarissa a lace bandeau.

Clarissa held it close to the light. "It matches the dress, I see."

"Of course it does. Her ladyship likes everything she wears to look right."

Half an hour later, Clarissa studied her reflection in the tall looking glass next to the dressing table, amazed that she could look so elegant. She touched a curl cascading over the bandeau and said, "You *should* be a lady's maid. It is such a waste to have you making beds and emptying chamber pots. Perhaps her ladyship will recommend you to one of her friends."

Millie looked panic stricken. "Do not breathe a word of this to Lady Fairfax, I beg of you. It is but a fancy I have. I lack the skills it takes to maintain a lady's clothes. I can't even sew properly."

"I could teach you."

Millie shook her head. "You mean well, miss, but after a day's work, I barely have the strength to crawl into bed."

It occurred to Clarissa that to Millie it was not necessary for her wish to come true. Dreaming about it was an end in itself.

* * *

Marcus stood patiently while Hillman adjusted his cravat. Finding Clarissa was staying at Fairfax Towers had proved unsettling. He wondered if she was there as an employee or a guest. It was hard to say. If the former, his mother's behavior toward her was inappropriate to say the least.

He was still mulling this over when he encountered his mother at the foot of the stairs.

"Dinner should have been served five minutes ago, Marcus. What on earth do you do with your time?"

Marcus touched his neckwear. "Hillman had difficulty getting my cravat to lie right. You know what a fusspot he is."

His mother regarded the result with a jaundiced eye. "Hillman's shortcomings are not my concern. I want to warn you that Clarissa will be joining us at dinner."

"*Warn* me? Why? Do you think the shock will kill me? *Really*, Mother!"

"Of course not. I wanted to impress upon you that she is no longer the little girl you used to call Gnat and to treat her accordingly."

Marcus considered her attitude extremely irritating. "I am well aware of that. I danced with her at the ball, did I not?"

"Only two days after you pulled her into a pig wallow. Such a cavalier attitude will no longer be tolerated. Try to be especially charming during dinner." Lady Fairfax rolled her eyes. "God knows, you could do with the practice."

"Make up your mind, Mother. It was not long ago you accused me of being too charming."

"Under different circumstances, as well you know," she replied.

Marcus followed her into a small reception room, saying, "And how does one charm a tree-climbing young firebrand, do you suppose? Offer to—"

Marcus stopped in mid sentence and stared at Clarissa, his mouth agape. *Good heavens*, he thought. *What was Mother thinking, dressing her like that? That russet color becomes her, I suppose, but the way her hair is dressed and those outrageous black things dangling from her ears are far too sophisticated for one of her tender years.*

"Remove the leaves from her hair?" Clarissa rejoined.

"Hmm?" Marcus was completely lost.

Lady Fairfax sighed. "Perhaps I ask too much of you, Marcus. But do pull yourself together and at least try to be civil."

"All that roistering you do in town is to blame," Lord Fairfax inserted. "If you put in an early night once in a while, you would be a lot better off."

"Yes, Father," Marcus, said, offering complete surrender in the hope it would end the matter.

Lady Fairfax smiled. "Good. Now let us go into dinner."

Marcus turned to the unfamiliar, sophisticated-looking Clarissa and offered her his arm. "Allow me," he said, hoping he had added the requisite amount of charm to the tone of his voice.

"Stand aside, son," Lord Fairfax said, his arm crooked to receive Clarissa's hand. "Let an expert show you how it is done."

Chapter 15

Mrs. Gates closed the oven door on the Christmas goose and, looking very pleased, said to Clarissa, "Be sure to keep the fire going, dear, and the bird should be cooked in plenty of time for dinner."

Clarissa nodded then went into the scullery, returning with a cauliflower.

"Plenty of time for that, dear," Mrs. Gates said. "As special treat, we shall take tea before we see to the rest of the dinner. I think we have earned it."

Glad of the opportunity to sit down, Clarissa gratefully accepted the cup of tea Mrs. Gates poured for her. She sipped the aromatic beverage and cast an appreciative glance at all the familiar things surrounding her: the china displayed on the shelves of an elaborately carved Welsh dresser, cast iron pots on the hearth, yellow earthenware mixing bowls nested on the kitchen table waiting to be used, and, hanging from the ceiling, dried herbs and stringed onions harvested from the kitchen garden.

It is as if my stay at Fairfax Towers was but a dream.

Clarissa had seldom encountered Marcus in the days following his arrival at Fairfax Towers. He had spent his days ranging the countryside, a pack of excited spaniels for companionship. In the evenings, he had a constant stream of invitations to dine with the local gentry.

Clarissa rather suspected that most of his hosts had a daughter or two to dangle under his nose. As she sipped her tea, she choked back a giggle. Evidently Marcus had deemed facing the husband hunters preferable to risking another evening making a cake of himself at his parent's table.

The Christmas dinner proved to be a great success. Mrs. Gates received special praise for the roast goose with the chestnut stuffing. Clarissa found the silver sixpence in her portion of Christmas pudding, a clear sign, according to her mother, that the year of eighteen hundred and thirteen would prove to be most propitious for Clarissa.

Long after the holly boughs and the mistletoe had been taken down, Clarissa looked back on that day with pleasure. Everyone had been so agreeable. Even her parents had not exchanged one cross word.

For the rest of the winter, life in the Carter household proved uneventful. Clarissa feared lest a monotonous existence was all she could expect for the rest of her days.

Early in March, fate, in the guise of an unexpected storm, proved otherwise. Her father came home one evening looking very grave. "Lord Fairfax took a spill from his horse this morning," he said.

"Good heavens," Mrs. Carter replied. "By the look on your face, he must have suffered a grievous injury."

"That is the irony of it. His lordship did not suffer any broken bones when he fell, but unfortunately he hit his head on a rock and was rendered unconscious for a while."

Mrs. Carter smiled. "There you are, then. It could have been a lot worse."

Mr. Carter shook his head. "Would that it were so. If you recall, there was a sudden storm this morning. It did not last long, but the wind was cold and the rain turned to sleet. Luckily, his lordship's horse returned to the stable and a search party was sent out to look for him. Otherwise I shudder to think of the consequences. As it is, the poor man was in a terrible state when they found him—soaking wet and frozen to the bone."

Mrs. Carter clutched her throat. "This has been a dreadful winter. Her poor ladyship must be frantic."

"I agree," Clarissa inserted. "When I was staying at Fairfax Towers, his lordship had a brief bout of coughing. Nothing serious, but he could not convince her ladyship of that. She insisted on sending for Dr. Russell. It appears that most of his lordship's colds are inclined to settle on his chest."

"Then heaven help him," Mrs. Carter rejoined.

"I should like to offer her my services," Clarissa said.

"In my opinion, that would be most presumptuous," her father replied. "You should remember your place."

Mrs. Carter looked thoughtful. "Under the circumstances, Edwin, my dear, I am afraid I cannot agree."

Mr. Carter frowned. "Oh? And what circumstances might they be?"

"Lady Fairfax has accorded Clarissa every consideration, has she not?"

"One might say so."

"*Might?* No other girl in this village can boast of such."

"I fail to see how that has any bearing on the matter."

"Do you not see, Edwin? It has *everything* to do with it. If Clarissa does not show *some* concern regarding his lordship's plight, she might very well be taken for a coldhearted, unfeeling ingrate."

Mr. Carter's lips quirked. "Coldhearted and unfeeling, eh?"

"And an ingrate."

"Dear me, that will never do. Very well, write your note, Clarissa, and I will see that it reaches her ladyship."

The following morning, Clarissa handed her father the note she had written. Two days later she received a reply from Lady Fairfax via her father.

"As I feared, his lordship has come down with a severe case of lung fever, and it would seem that Lady Fairfax would very much like to avail herself of your services." He seemed puzzled by this. "Heaven knows what possible use you might be in such a situation. Nevertheless, pack a valise right away. Her ladyship is sending a carriage for you first thing tomorrow morning."

On arriving at Fairfax Towers, Clarissa was relieved to see that she had been allotted the same chamber as on her previous stay. She found something reassuring in the familiar surroundings.

Not used to having others handle her things, rather than

wait for a chambermaid to do it for her, she hung her clothes in the massive mahogany dresser immediately, then neatly folded her unmentionables and put them in an adjoining chest of drawers.

She was about to take a quick peek in the tall looking glass to be sure that her dress hem needed no adjusting, when Sanders the butler knocked on her door to inform her that her presence was required in the master's chambers.

Mystified by such a request, Clarissa followed Sanders down the hallway. She expected to be taken to his lordship's sitting room and was taken aback when ushered into Lord Fairfax's bedchamber.

At first, she was struck by how the color green dominated the room, and then became distracted by the sound of labored breathing. Her gaze was drawn to a large bed with an ornately carved headboard that reached up to meet the elaborate ceiling molding. Dwarfed by its size, Lord Fairfax lay beneath the headboard, his head propped up on a pile of pillows.

At the far side of the bed, Lady Fairfax sat leaning forward on the edge of a chair, her gaze firmly fixed on her husband's face, as if willing him to get better.

Clarissa turned and realized that the butler had withdrawn, leaving her to make her own presence known. She hesitated for a moment then coughed. Lady Fairfax gave a start, then rose to greet her.

"My dear girl. It is good of you to come at such short notice," she said, briefly clasping Clarissa's hands in hers.

"Not at all, my lady," Clarissa replied, both surprised and touched by the gesture. "After all the kindness you have shown me, it was the very least I could do. Perhaps for starters I could watch over Lord Fairfax while you take a much needed rest?"

"Bless you, no, child. I do not wish to leave him, but bring over a chair and sit by my side. Your company will comfort me."

Clarissa sat next to Lady Fairfax and watched with alarm as his lordship seemingly fought for every breath. "Has there been any improvement in his lordship's condition?" she asked, hoping against hope that such was the case.

Lady Fairfax choked back a sob. "Alas, no. None of the usual elixirs or poultices seem to help, and the doctor has cupped him several times, to no avail. All one can do is hope and pray."

Clarissa took the liberty of patting her hand. "I am terribly sorry. His lordship is such a kind gentleman. Have Marcus—I mean, Lord Ridley and Mr. Ridley been informed?"

"Yes, they have. Both of them should arrive early in the afternoon, weather allowing. And in private you have my permission to refer to them by their first names. I believe you have done so most of your life."

"That is true, I am ashamed to say. Neither one saw fit to tell me it was not the proper thing to do."

Lady Fairfax looked rueful. "I think in part that some of the blame could be laid at my door."

Not knowing how to react to such a remark, Clarissa made no reply.

"Before I married Lord Fairfax, I was simply Miss Mary Elizabeth Louise Wilson. My father was a kindly gentleman and my sister Gertrude and I were raised in an atmosphere of love and laughter."

"As were Marcus and John. Both were incredibly kind to me when I was a little girl," Clarissa rejoined. "It never occurred to me before, but I see now that in some families, kindness and happiness are a sort of legacy passed down through the generations."

"*Exactly.* These were the values with which my sister and I were raised. Therefore, in choosing our friends, and, later, our husbands, we were encouraged to choose these qualities over rank and riches." She smiled and added, "Marrying the heir to an earldom was the furthest thing from my mind."

"Everyone says it was a love match."

"Everyone is right. I married a man every bit as kind and as considerate as my father—and now"—her voice broke—"I fear I am losing him."

"Dear, dear, Lady Fairfax, I pray that you are mistaken."

Lady Fairfax took a washcloth from a bowl on the nightstand and, after wringing out the excess water, wiped her husband's brow. "I have not left his side for but a moment or two at a time, since he was put to bed."

"Forgive me for asking, but is his lordship likely to waken?"

"Yes, thank heavens. He does but sleep. I expect him to do so within the hour."

"I know this is most presumptuous of me, but I think that in the meantime, you should take the opportunity to bathe and put on your prettiest dress. It does neither of you any good for him to see you looking less than your best."

Lady Fairfax looked down at her stained and rumpled dress as if seeing it for the first time, then shot Clarissa a look of utter dismay. "Why, I look like one of those filthy creatures that go from village to village stealing chickens. How could I not have noticed?"

"All your concern was focused on his lordship's plight."

"Even so, I should have exercised more care. Seeing me in this sorry state, he most likely thinks that his demise is imminent. In which case, he is apt to give up the struggle."

"Besides which, your complete disregard for your own well-being is bound to give your sons cause for alarm. I am sure you would not wish this."

"You are such a wise young thing. I shall put my abigail through her paces and return as quickly as possible. If his lordship should wake up, or show any signs of worsening, see that I am informed. I shall return in my shift, if need be."

When Lady Fairfax returned, Clarissa noticed that although her appearance was considerably improved, there were dark circles under her eyes. She convinced her to lie down on the daybed, citing that she would be of no use to his lordship were she to collapse from exhaustion.

"Should his lordship so much as roll on his side, I shall let you know."

"Very well, I will lie down, but doubt I shall close my eyes. My goodness, Clarissa, you are a bossy creature."

Contrary to what she thought, Lady Fairfax fell asleep almost immediately. As luck would have it, his lordship did not wake up for another hour.

Clarissa left the room so as not to intrude on their privacy. As she closed the chamber door, she gave a satisfied smile on hearing Lord Fairfax say, "Mary, my darling, you are still the most beautiful woman I have ever encountered."

Chapter 16

Lady Fairfax had just spoon-fed Lord Fairfax the last drop of beef broth that he would accept for his lunch when Marcus and John arrived at the house. They rushed immediately to their father's side, anxious to see how he was.

Tired from the ablutions performed by his manservant and the effort of drinking the hot broth administered by his wife, he lay back on his pillow as limp as a rag doll. Even so, for the benefit of his sons, he put on a brave front.

With a wry smile he looked them over and said, "You make a fine pair of ruffians, I must say. Of a certainty, neither one of you would be the worse for a good scrubbing and a change of clothes. Come over here and give your father a hug."

His voice was barely above a whisper, and Marcus and John leaned over him in order to hear what he was saying. Surprised by the request, both of them hastened to comply. With the typical reserve of an English gentleman, their father had not made such a demand of them since they had outgrown the need for leading strings.

"You were both good boys, and have turned out to be fine young men. Marcus, it would be a relief to your mother and me if you were to follow John's example and marry."

"I would be only too happy to oblige. Unfortunately, Father, I have yet to meet the right girl."

"Pah! She is probably right under your nose, if you would take the trouble to look."

"Pray do not be too critical of Marcus," John inserted. "Girls such as Althea are few and far between."

Lord Fairfax looked fondly on John. "Your mother and I are mindful of this. We are both very grateful to you for giving us Althea for a daughter-in-law, and of course our beautiful grandson. Did you bring them along?"

John shook his head. "Alas, no. I did not wish to risk it. God knows your mishap is a prime example of the dangers one can face in braving the elements."

"Oh quite," Lord Fairfax replied. "A wise decision, to be sure."

He was suddenly seized by a fit of coughing. Marcus raised his head and held a glass of water to his lips. His lordship took a few sips then sank back on the pillows, visibly weakened by the coughing bout. "You will forgive me if I ask you both to leave for the present," he gasped. "I am feeling rather tired."

"But of course, Father," Marcus replied. "John and I intend to meet in the library as soon as we have changed our clothes. Please send for us when it suits you."

On walking into the hallway, the last person Marcus and John expected to meet was Clarissa Carter.

"Hello there," John said. "What on earth are you doing here?"

"As you can see, Clarissa," Marcus said. "Brother John is as tactless as ever, but I see his point. Why *are* you here? Surely, under the circumstances, not to sew for our mother?"

"Of course not. I am here because Lady Fairfax sent for me. She is desirous of company while keeping vigil at his lordship's bedside. I think it gives her solace."

"I rather think that our mother has formed an attachment to you, Clarissa," Marcus said. "I find it most singular, considering the difference in your ages."

"Perhaps she sees in Clarissa the daughter she never had," John suggested. "After all, Clarissa was the closest thing to a sister that we had."

Clarissa laughed. "Come now, John. I seem to remember the word *Gnat* being bandied about in reference to me, but sister? *Never!*"

"Clarissa has a point."

"Fie, Marcus. And you have the temerity to call *me* tactless?"

"Now that you have arrived, perhaps Lady Fairfax has no

further need of my company."

Lady Fairfax took that moment to open the chamber door and say, "Ah, there you are, Clarissa. Have you eaten?"

"Yes, thank you, your ladyship."

"Good. Lord Fairfax has dropped off to sleep and I would welcome some company."

"Does that answer your question, Clarissa?" Marcus asked.

"What question might that be?" Lady Fairfax wanted to know.

"Clarissa was just wondering if, since John and I are here, her services were still required."

"Of course they are. The very idea. Clarissa is a veritable rock."

"A rock, eh?" John parried. "Ought Marcus and I to feel snubbed?"

"Only if you wish it," Lady Fairfax replied. Then, as soon as Clarissa entered the bedchamber, she blew them a kiss and closed the door.

Marcus and John were starting on their second brandy when Sanders gave a discreet knock on the library door and announced that their presence was requested in Lord Fairfax's bedchamber. "I fear his lordship has taken a turn for the worse."

"Has Dr. Russell been summoned?"

"His lordship decided yesterday that he preferred to die in peace rather than, as he put it, suffer more indignity at the hands of that incompetent"

John sighed. "I cannot say as I blame him, but it must be terribly hard on Mother."

"I refuse to stand by and do nothing," Marcus said. "I shall ride to London this instant and bring back a more able doctor, even if I have to bind and gag the fellow to get him here."

"Begging your pardon, my lord," Sanders interjected. "I am afraid it is too late for that. I advise you to repair to his lordship's chamber with all speed. He is fading fast."

Marcus and John leaped out of their chairs, slammed their brandy glasses down, and rushed out of the room, coming perilously close to knocking Sanders off his feet in the process.

They entered their father's bedchamber and saw that their mother was kneeling by his side, her hand pressed to his cheek. Clarissa stood by the window facing away from the bed, trying not to intrude.

Clarissa turned, then came to them and clasped each of their hands in turn. "I am so sorry," she said.

Marcus saw a tear glisten on her cheek and nodded, moved by her concern for them.

"Now that you are here to comfort Lady Fairfax I am sure she will be all right. But just in case, I shall be directly outside," she said, and curtsied to them.

They nodded, then went directly to their mother's side. Marcus laid his hand on her shoulder. She shot him a brief glance and, with a constrained smile, turned and kissed Lord Fairfax on the cheek.

"Open your eyes, darling," she whispered, giving his shoulder a gentle shake. "Marcus and John are here."

Lord Fairfax did not stir.

Marcus helped her to her feet and held her close. "You should have sent for us sooner, Mother. We should have been here for you."

She sighed. "I did not think it necessary. I suppose I refused to think the unthinkable." She clutched his sleeve. "Marcus, what am I going to do? I cannot conceive of a life that does not include your father."

Marcus stroked her hair. "John and I will see you through this."

"Of course you will, darling. Please forgive my unseemly outburst" Composed once more, she stepped back from the bed to make way for them.

Marcus bent over and kissed his lordship's brow, then stepped aside for John. His brother immediately clasped the dying man's hand and stared intently at him.

John is not taking this too well, Marcus thought. *He devours Father with his gaze. It's as if he thinks there might be some aspect of his face he might have missed. Or, perhaps, fears the memory of it might fade with time.*

John kissed the earl on the cheek and backed away, wiping at a tear with his index finger.

Lady Fairfax resumed her place by the bed, and Lord Fairfax opened his eyes and reached for her hand.

"He is awake," she said, a tremor of excitement in her voice. She leaned over and kissed him.

He, in turn, kissed her hand, murmuring, "Just one more kiss, my heart's blood."

Marcus noticed that the next kiss his mother bestowed upon his father was warm and tender, the sort of kiss that lovers share. He realized that for her, his father's death would be devastating.

When the kiss was over, she laid her head on his chest and he stroked her hair, a look of utter contentment on his face. "My Mary. The most beautiful girl in all of Surrey," he murmured, closing his eyes for the last time.

Chapter 17

As Marcus feared, Lady Fairfax was extremely distraught over the death of his father. At first, she refused to leave his bedside. Once persuaded to do so, she sought refuge in her own room and refused to see anyone.

Clarissa was retained for another day, then sent home. Mrs. Gates immediately invited her into the kitchen, ostensibly for a glass of milk and some sugar biscuits, but lost no time in pumping her for all the news pertaining to Lord Fairfax's demise.

"There is not much to say. Poor Lady Fairfax is inconsolable, of course."

"I heard she has taken to her bed. It is to be hoped that she pulls herself together in time for the funeral tomorrow."

Clarissa sensed a trace of criticism in the housekeeper's tone and hastened to Lady Fairfax's defense. "Of course Lady Fairfax will attend the funeral. She is not the sort to shirk her duty."

Clarissa accompanied her parents to St. Martin's for Lord Fairfax's funeral, wearing a dress and matching cape of a rich black crepe. The material had come from one of Grandmother Carter's voluminous mourning dresses.

The Carters drove to the church in a dog cart, a roomy hand-me-down from Mr. Carter's brother, Henry. At the graveside, Clarissa and her family stood a respectful distance from the chief mourners. Marcus and John flanked Lady Fairfax on either side.

It distressed Clarissa to see how thin and gaunt she looked. *I doubt a morsel of food has passed her lips since her husband died*, she thought.

Afterward, she joined the line of sympathizers and offered the bereaved woman her condolences. Lady Fairfax put a hand on Clarissa's shoulder and from behind the thick veil covering her face, she said, "Please come back, Clarissa. I was most upset when I found they had sent you away."

"I would be honored to do so whenever it pleases you, Lady Fairfax."

"Then tomorrow afternoon?"

"Certainly." Clarissa curtsied, and moved on to Marcus. He attempted a smile, but it quickly died. She thought he looked terribly sad.

Poor Marcus is so busy handling everyone else's grief he has no time to address his own, she thought.

"Welcome back to the fold, Miss Carter," he said. "I am thinking that it is a heavy burden for such young shoulders to carry."

"It is hard to lose a loved one," she replied. "Especially someone as kindly as Lord Fairfax. I know I still miss dear Grandmother Carter most dreadfully. I find great solace in remembering the happy times we shared."

Marcus bowed to her. "It is comforting to know that my mother will have such a wise and understanding young lady to keep her company."

On the way home, her father said, "So you are going back to Fairfax Towers?"

"Lady Fairfax was kind enough to ask me."

"I hope you are aware of the significance of such a move," he replied, his brow knitted with concern.

"Significance? I am not sure I understand."

"I rather thought not. To all intents and purposes, Lady Fairfax has asked you to become her companion. That means, barring an inability to get along, that you will most likely retain the position until the day that one of you dies. Are you sure this is what you want to do with your life?"

"It would be a good life, Papa. Lady Fairfax is most amiable."

"In some ways, it could be a very good life. You would never want for anything and would be close to home. This might not be the case if you were to become a governess." He pulled on the reins to slow down the horse. "On the other hand, there is a strong possibility that you will be giving up the opportunity of finding a husband and having children of your own."

"Pish posh, Edwin," Mrs. Carter interjected. "I think that living at Fairfax Towers would afford Clarissa a wonderful opportunity to make a brilliant marriage—perhaps to someone like that nice Mr. Thistlethwaite."

"I have no intention of marrying anyone, Mama."

"You are too young to be making that sort of decision. Tell her, Edwin. I declare, I have never heard of anything so unnatural in my life."

"It is pointless for me to say anything on the matter. I am sure that if the right young man were to offer for Clarissa, she would marry him in a trice."

"Yes. I suppose she would," Mrs. Carter replied, apparently satisfied with this answer, for she remained silent for the rest of the drive home.

The first thing to catch Clarissa's eye on returning to Fairfax Towers was how somber the footmen looked, with their magnificent green and gold liveries replaced by suits of black.

For the first six months, life at Fairfax Towers was uneventful. On assuming the title of earl, Marcus's visits to his ancestral home became more frequent, but since the Prince Regent's affairs had become more pressing, the responsibility of managing the estate fell to Mr. Carter.

Lady Fairfax remained in seclusion and according to custom neither entertained nor accepted the invitations of others. However, she resumed her afternoon sewing sessions with Clarissa. As they worked on their needlework, the lady would sometimes discuss her feelings regarding her husband's death.

One day she said, "It was the strangest thing, Clarissa. All my married life I have felt young and desirable, the focus of my husband's utter love and devotion. It was not until I became a widow that I realized I had become an old woman."

Clarissa was tempted to argue the point but refrained, realizing that a response was neither needed nor desired.

"You have no idea how angry it makes me. God, how I miss him!" Lady Fairfax exclaimed, her eyes glistening with tears. "He had no right to risk what we had by venturing forth in such weather."

By September, Lady Fairfax seemed to have worked out her feelings regarding her husband's death. In any case, she no longer railed against her loss and, as if a fog had lifted, began to review her own situation. As a result she requested a meeting with Marcus in the library.

While waiting for her to arrive for the appointment, Marcus passed the time looking at the gardens through the library window and happened to catch sight of Clarissa walking across the lawn. *Carter's daughter carries herself with more grace than most highborn ladies that I know*, he thought. *But I cannot say as I like that purpose in her step. Of a certainty, the chit is up to no good.*

Lady Fairfax chose that moment to enter the library. Marcus invited her to sit in a wing chair covered in dark green leather. He sat next to her on a matching chair and waited to hear what she had to say.

"I want to apologize for the great inconvenience I have caused you. I cannot imagine what I was thinking all these months," she said.

"What inconvenience would that be, Mother?"

"Intruding upon your privacy. I should have moved to the Dower House months ago."

"Nonsense," Marcus rejoined. "If you leave, the servants are apt to let things slide. Lord knows, the way Prinny keeps me hopping, I am not home as often as I would like to be."

"Dancing attendance on that silly man to the detriment of your own affairs cannot be easy. No matter how many plans he has drawn for the remodeling of the Pavilion, I doubt he will ever be truly satisfied with the outcome."

Marcus refrained from telling her that fussing over plans for the Pavilion in Brighton ranked low on the list of duties he performed for prince and country.

He shuddered to think how she would react if she found out about his intriguing and plotting against the French or his occasional trips into enemy territory, which, of necessity, had increased when John dropped out of the spy business. *She would have my guts for garters if she so much as suspected I had put her baby in the face of danger.*

"Unfortunately, you could very well be right," he countered. "As with all perfectionists, His Royal Highness is difficult to please. In any case, if you have no objections, I should like you to stay on at the house."

"For the time being, then." She stood up to go.

"Must you go so soon?"

"I would rather. I should like to take a nap before dinner."

When his mother left, Marcus decided to go after Clarissa. On nearing the oak tree, he let out a groan. Since Clarissa was attempting to hang from a tree branch by her feet, it was plain to see that she was wearing his breeches under the dark gray dress she had on. Not having perfected the art of hanging by one's feet, she had her hands firmly planted on the ground.

Once a gnat, always a gnat. Damn her. I threw those breeches into the bushes. She must have boiled them to get the mud out.

"You might as well give up, young lady. You are not going to pull it off," he called to her. Instantly he regretted it, because, startled by the sound of his voice, she lost her balance and landed in a heap at the foot of the tree.

He rushed over and helped her to her feet. "Are you hurt?" he asked, very much concerned. "I did not mean to frighten you."

She looked aggrieved. "I would have managed it, but for that."

"I beg to differ. The branch is a trifle thick to lock on to with one's feet. Although why you would want to is beyond me."

"Curiosity. You and John used to do it all the time, but you would never let me even try."

"Clarissa, you are lucky you are tall enough for your hands to reach the ground. Otherwise right now you would be nursing a cracked pate." As an afterthought, he asked, "You had no right to go back for those breeches. I made it clear that there was to be no more tree climbing."

Clarissa shook her head. "I mean no disrespect, but you

...id *we* would no longer climb trees together."

"Is this more of your sophistry?"

"On my honor 'tis true."

Without thinking the matter through, Marcus blurted, "Hanging by one's knees is a lot easier. I will help you do it, but you must promise to make it a onetime thing."

Clarissa's face lit up. "Once will be enough. I just want to satisfy my curiosity. I had to watch while John and you seemed to have such a jolly time. You have no idea how frustrating that was."

He marveled at her youthful enthusiasm. *She is such an innocent. It would never occur to her that the years have turned a childhood prank into a scandalous proposition. And why is it I cannot say no to her, and continue to indulge her whimsies?*

"Here goes," he called, climbing up to the branch that Clarissa had used previously. She was quick to join him.

"Hook your knees over the branch and I'll hold while you bend backward," he said, hoping she would cry off.

She followed his instructions without a moment's hesitation. As she lowered, her hair fell free, spilling to the ground in a cascade of fiery curls.

Give Clarissa her due, he thought, *her hair looks magnificent with the sun shining on it.*

He came to earth when she called out, "You may let go."

"Are you certain?" he asked, embarrassed for harboring such thoughts.

"Yes. But hurry, please. The blood is rushing to my head."

Marcus loosened his grip on her waist but kept contact with her clothing. "Is it as much fun as you thought it would be?" he asked.

"Oh, yes. But I should like to come up now."

"Give me your hand, then."

As he pulled her up, her face glowed. Once seated on the branch, she said, "It was most exhilarating. Most of the excitement came from the danger involved. Thank you so much, Marcus—or perhaps now you are the earl, I should not call you that anymore."

"Perhaps," he said. "But then I would have to call you Miss Carter, and old habits die hard."

He regretted the words as soon as he uttered them. *Why am I always engaged in some sort of deception with this girl?* He wondered. Then it dawned on him that the shortcoming probably harked back to his childhood. Old habits, he decided, did not die at all.

Chapter 18

During dinner that evening, Marcus treated Clarissa with polite formality. But this was nothing new. *It is as if Marcus my friend and Marcus Ridley, Earl of Fairfax, are two completely different people who just happen to share the same body*, she mused.

Marcus announced he was returning to Brighton. "If you wish me to drop you off at Camberly to visit John and his family, I will gladly wait a few days for you to get ready. After all, you have not seen Percy since last Christmas. You would not recognize him, he has grown so."

Lady Fairfax shook her head. "Thank you for asking me, darling, but I am not ready to venture forth. Perhaps you can persuade Althea to bring the baby here before the weather changes."

"Perhaps," he replied. "You know, Mother, Percy will not be a baby for much longer. His nursemaid is hard put to keep up with him; he is toddling all over the place. Are you sure about not going?"

"Next time, Marcus."

"In that case, I shall leave tomorrow."

Clarissa noticed that he was remarkably quiet for the rest of the meal.

Winter came, and it seemed to Clarissa that it made very little difference one way or the other. At Fairfax Towers, the monotony of their daily routine was varied, and then only slightly, by the occasional visits they received from Marcus.

When her nineteenth birthday rolled around in early December, Clarissa stayed overnight at her parents' house and was treated to a celebratory dinner.

While Mrs. Gates served the fruitcake she had baked for

the occasion, Mrs. Carter voiced her dissatisfaction over the way things were going at Fairfax Towers.

"One would think that the new earl would invite some of his friends to Fairfax Towers. After all, it has been nine months since his father passed away."

"I do not think that is likely to happen until his mother's outlook improves," Mr. Carter inserted. "Her grief casts a pall over the house. I am sure Clarissa will attest to that."

Clarissa nodded. "Lady Fairfax suffered a great loss, but she is coming around. One has to take things day by day."

Mrs. Carter sniffed. "It is not much of a life for a young girl. Of course, one does not expect Lady Fairfax to entertain for the first year, but it would not be untoward for the new earl to invite his friends for a quiet weekend. That nice Mr. Thistlethwaite, for instance."

"There is no cause for concern on that account, Beatrice," Mr. Carter rejoined. "According to the newspapers, our Lord Fairfax entertains his friends quite often at the London establishment."

"That does not do our Clarissa any good."

"It may come as a surprise, dear, but I hardly think that providing our daughter with a husband is a priority with him."

"Please," Clarissa remonstrated. "I find this conversation most distasteful."

"La. Such airs and graces we have acquired since taking up residence at the great house," Mrs. Carter replied tartly.

"Come now, Beatrice. Let us not spoil Clarissa's day."

Mrs. Carter gave her head an angry toss. "To be sure, I do not know what you mean, Mr. Carter." She turned her attention to Clarissa. "Tell me, child. Did your Lady Fairfax see fit to give you anything for your birthday?"

"Yes, Mama, she was most generous. She gave me two lengths of muslin and the accompanying trimming to make into dresses for next summer. A pale blue dotted Swiss and a very fine Indian in a peach color."

"Just fancy," Mrs. Carter replied, clasping her bosom. "Her ladyship must hold you in very high regard, Clarissa. Very high indeed. Did you hear that, Edwin? *Two* lengths of muslin, no less!"

"It is a positive sign that perhaps by summer, her ladyship will have shed her widow's weeds," Mr. Carter observed. "I must admit that I am tired of seeing Clarissa in black or gray all the time."

Marcus came home for Christmas, so Clarissa received permission to go home for the holiday. This year it was Mrs. Carter who found the silver sixpence in her piece of Christmas pudding.

She gazed fondly at Clarissa, saying, "I have such a good feeling about this."

Mr. Carter merely shook his head.

As Easter approached, Marcus suggested that they should celebrate the holiday with John and his family.

Lady Fairfax demurred, and Marcus took her to task. "Father has been gone for over a year. It is time to get on with your life."

"That is for me to decide."

"To be honest, Mother, I do not think you are capable of deciding. I think if I were to let the matter ride for another year, your answer would still be the same. I think it is about time you gave some thought to your family."

Lady Fairfax looked surprised. "My family?"

"Yes, your family. We do exist. Percy needs his grandmother and John and I want our mother back. We both miss her terribly."

Lady Fairfax covered her face with her hands. "Oh dear. I have been dreadfully self-indulgent, have I not?"

"Dreadfully," he said, pulling her close and kissing her forehead. She stood with her head resting on his shoulder for a full minute before pulling away.

"When do you wish me to be ready?"

"The end of the week, if you can manage it. And, Mother?"

"Hmm?"

"Do not pack anything black. It is time for a transition to other colors. You do not wish to frighten Percy, now do you?"

She looked rueful. "Oh, dear, do I look that dreadful?"

When Marcus left, she dropped by the sewing room to

apprise Clarissa of what had taken place, finishing with, "So you can see I was chastised thoroughly."

"It will be wonderful for you to visit your family, your ladyship," Clarissa said, snipping a thread on a tiny garment earmarked for a dairymaid's baby.

"You will be going, too."

"If it is all the same to you, Lady Fairfax, I would rather not. You will be busy with your family, and I would be in the way. In the meantime, there is plenty of sewing for me to do."

"Hmm. I see your point. And, of course you will want to spend Easter with your family. Very well, you need not accompany me this time, but it will not always be the case."

Clarissa curtsied. "Nor would I wish it to be, my lady. I deem it an honor and a pleasure to be of service to such a kind and gracious lady."

Lady Fairfax was amused. "La, Clarissa, such a pretty speech. You have the tongue of a courtier."

To Clarissa's surprise and gratification, Lady Fairfax leaned over and kissed her on the cheek. She could not remember the last time her own mother had made such a gesture.

To Clarissa's delight, Lady Fairfax returned from her visit to Seaview House fully restored in spirit She greeted each day with enthusiasm; went about her duties with a spring to her step and, more often than not, could be heard humming a cheerful tune.

When summer came, she stopped wearing the dark colors reserved for the final stages of the mourning period and declared herself ready to resume her social obligations. Clarissa was putting the final touches to the dress she had made with the Swiss muslin she received for her birthday when Lady Fairfax dropped a bombshell.

"Since my son is disinclined to make a serious effort to find a wife, it is up to me to do it for him," she said. "Why, even the *London Times* mentions that he eschews such functions as would enable him to meet a suitable bride. Instead, he divides his time between hobnobbing with his cronies at such places as White's or Boodles and haring all over the countryside in his curricle with his friend Bertram Thistlethwaite in tow."

Her words felled Clarissa. Unable to reply, she continued to ply her needle to the flounce she was sewing.

"To this end, I should like to hold a house party sometime in August, if I can persuade Marcus to forgo his idle pleasures long enough to attend."

Chapter 19

"I cannot believe my good fortune," Lady Fairfax said to Clarissa when they were strolling through the rose garden late in June. "Marcus has agreed to a house party on the second week in August."

Clarissa felt as though the last nail had been driven into the lid of her coffin.

"But he has one condition."

I do not find that in the least surprising, Clarissa thought *Marcus is past master at attaching conditions to his favors.*

"Really? And what might that be, your ladyship?"

"That if my quest to find him a bride turns out to be as big a fiasco as my other attempts, I must promise never to try again. I had better send out my invitations before he begins to have second thoughts on the matter and refuses altogether."

"I would be happy to help in any way I can," Clarissa murmured.

"Bless you, child," Lady Fairfax rejoined. "You are my good right arm."

As the guests arrived at Fairfax Towers the second Monday in August, Clarissa made a point of assessing every young lady in their midst who seemed to be of an age to marry. Clarissa counted six. It would seem that Lady Fairfax intended to make the most of a last-ditch effort to acquire a daughter-in-law.

All six girls were attractive, in their own way. Clarissa deemed Miss Dulcie Ponsonby, a brown-haired, blue-eyed beauty, to be much too short for Marcus. Both Miss Lorna Everett and Miss Henrietta Ross were incessant gigglers and would not interest him in the slightest.

A brief conversation with Lady Diana Clendenin left Clarissa firmly convinced that the girl had the intelligence of a cauliflower. On the other hand, Clarissa could not remember ever having met any females as breathtakingly beautiful as the Misses Charlotte Forbes and Rowena Arden.

Both girls were tall and slender and proud of carriage, but completely dissimilar in looks. Miss Forbes had fair hair and eyes the color of forget-me-nots, whereas Miss Arden reminded Clarissa of a sleek cat with her raven-black tresses and jade-green eyes. It occurred to Clarissa that with a little research, Lady Fairfax could have cut down considerably on her guest list.

As she surmised, Marcus accorded the gigglers, Misses Everett and Ross, as little attention as good manners would allow. Ditto Lady Diana the ninnyhammer.

To Clarissa's surprise, Marcus engaged in considerable dialog with the petite Dulcie Ponsonby. But when it came to those diamonds of the first water, Charlotte Forbes and Rowena Arden, Clarissa thought Marcus played a dangerous game, flirting outrageously with one, then the other, and back again.

She stood next to Bertie Thistlethwaite on the lawn one afternoon, watching Marcus make a big display of giving Rowena Arden an archery lesson. Her eyes widened in disbelief when Marcus enfolded the girl in his arms, ostensibly to teach her how to draw the bow.

"Marcus had better stop playing those silly games if he wishes to live to a ripe old age," Bertie whispered.

"What do you mean?" Clarissa whispered back.

"The gentleman who is glowering at him is her brother, William Arden."

"Oh? And who might he be?"

"Only the most skillful duelist in all of England. He is a nonpareil in both sword and pistol and, I have heard, has knocked many a belligerent senseless with his fists."

"But his lordship has yet to lose a duel," Clarissa replied. "Not that I like to think of him engaged in anything so dangerous."

"Marcus does not relish the pastime. Oh, he's good, mind you, but he only meets on the grass when challenged by a hothead who will not be talked out of it." Bertie nodded in William Arden's direction. "That gentleman, on the other hand, relishes the letting of another man's blood."

"I wonder what possessed Lady Fairfax to invite such a person."

"Bless her, she probably had no idea. It is the sort of gossip one is apt to hear at one's club, not in a withdrawing room."

"And the other young lady? Does she have a brother here also waiting to pounce on his lordship?"

Bertie grinned. "His lordship? That is the second time you've called him by his honorific. How circumspect of you, my dear. I am well aware that you and Marcus have been friends since childhood."

"Circumspection is an essential part of such a friendship, Mr. Thistlethwaite. I should hate to think that he would be embarrassed through any indiscretion of mine."

"Well said, Miss Carter, and yes, Miss Forbes does have a brother here, but since he has but fifteen years, he is not likely to go up against our foolhardy friend."

"That is a relief, I must say."

"I do not doubt that for one minute, Miss Carter," Bertie said, looking extremely arch. "If our mutual friend stopped still long enough to think things through, he would realize that the ideal wife for him has been right under his nose all along and send all the other young ladies packing."

Clarissa felt her face flame. "Fie, Mr. Thistlethwaite. That remark was uncalled for."

"But true. And if I did not think that you loved Marcus to the point of distraction, I would offer for you myself."

Good heavens, Clarissa thought. *Am I that transparent?*

She drew herself up with all the dignity she could muster and, keeping her voice as low as possible, replied, "Good day, sir. I refuse to stay and listen your nonsense any longer."

Bertie bowed to her with such a self-assured smile on his face, she was sorely tempted to slap him. She dipped him the briefest of curtsies and turned tail. It seemed to Clarissa that the time it took for her to traverse the hundred yards or so to the house would never end.

Unable to face Bertie Thistlethwaite and what she interpreted to be his knowing little smile, Clarissa did not go down to dinner that evening, claiming a headache for an excuse.

She was fearful that on further acquaintance, the other guests might prove to be as perceptive as Bertie Thistlethwaite and discover her love for their host. The following afternoon, rather than join them in their lawn games, she hied to a seldom used part of the garden and took refuge on a bench behind a hedge of ancient yews.

In spite of being in the shade, the air was balmy and what with the chirping of the sparrows and the droning of the bees, Clarissa nodded off to sleep. She was awakened by the sound of a feminine voice speaking in a breathy tone, which she recognized as Rowena Arden's.

"If I have to pretend ineptness at archery one more day, I think I shall scream," she said. "Besides, Papa, I do not think for a minute that your precious earl is deceived. He is having a fine time flitting between that whey-faced Charlotte Forbes and me. He reminds me of a honeybee among the flowers."

"No one said that catching an earl would be easy, but it is imperative that you do."

"Mr. Arden, I fear you degrade our daughter with your sordid little schemes." The older woman sounded querulous.

"Mrs. Arden, you might prefer to spend the rest of your days in debtor's prison, but I certainly do not," Mr. Arden rejoined.

Clarissa scarcely breathed in an effort not to be discovered. She did not like to eavesdrop, but, for Marcus's sake, felt she should.

"Mr. Arden, have you not learned one thing from your mistakes? You would rather risk our future trying to catch a rich earl for a son-in-law where better men have failed. You would be far wiser to settle for a nice country gentleman not quite so plump in the pocket." Clarissa heard her sob. "It is no different than you losing every penny we had by investing in the East

India Company."

"You cannot put all the blame on Father. Rowena was so sure she would have Fairfax eating out of her hand," William Arden inserted. "I think it is time for me to step in. Do as I say, and Rowena will be engaged within the hour."

William Arden started to reveal his plan, but had barely finished a sentence when he was bombarded by his family with objections.

"How dare you suggest that I should tear my dress? What if it is to no avail? Heaven knows I cannot afford to replace it," Rowena said, her voice declining into a whine.

"Pah! It is common knowledge that Fairfax would rather risk ostracism than give in to such a vulgar ruse," Mr. Arden blustered.

"Have you no regard for my baby's sensibilities? Oh, that I should have lived to see this day."

Clarissa presumed that, like her mother, Mrs. Arden would be clasping her bosom while passing such a remark.

"Let me start over, and please do me the goodness of not interrupting until I have finished speaking."

"All right. But I do not see what good it will do," Mr. Arden grumbled.

"Please, Father. We have established that after those footling lawn games, Marcus Ridley retires to his library, probably to imbibe some brandy, if I know anything about it."

"For goodness sake, son, *do* get on with it."

"Well, I do not intend for Rowena to dash in there willy-nilly, ripping her dress. God knows what sort of a pickle that would turn out to be. The man seems to have a special power over women."

Mrs. Arden began to whimper. "I do not like the sound of this. No. Not at all."

"Do be quiet and let William finish."

"My plan is for Rowena to rip her dress ever so slightly, as if his lordship got a little carried away, and to start screaming for help the minute she sets foot through the library door. We shall be right behind her demanding that he do the honorable thing."

"Out of the question. He will refuse, and will see to it we are not received in a house of any consequence ever again."

"You are mistaken, Father, for if I should call him out, the man knows that he faces certain death. Look at Rowena. Marriage to her is bound to have more appeal than death by my hand."

You do not know Marcus Ridley very well, Clarissa thought, *or you would not labor under such a delusion. He would suffer the tortures of the damned rather than submit to such a plot.*

"Well, let's hurry and let's get it over with before he takes it into his head to leave the library. If I have too much time to think, I will not be able to go through with this. It is far too risky."

Mrs. Arden sniffed. "That coming from a man who has beggared his family with his wild schemes."

Clarissa heard the sound of their feet crunching on the gravel path. She peeked around the hedge and saw that with Mrs. Arden in tow they were not moving particularly fast. She began running at an angle to them before swerving to the kitchen garden, where she entered the house through the servant's entrance.

While running down the flagstone hall, she bumped into Mrs. Cole. She grabbed the woman to prevent her from falling and continued running, calling out, "So sorry, Mrs. Cole, I will explain later." As she ran, she could hear the housekeeper mumbling to herself.

She bounded up two flights of the back stairs and as she was about to enter the library could hear the Ardens talking among themselves while coming up the grand staircase.

Realizing there was no time for explanations, Clarissa burst into the room to see Marcus staring at her, his brows raised in surprise.

Marcus thought that the pale blue muslin dress became her, and started to say so, when to his amazement she plopped down onto his lap and said, "No time for that."

It was all very well for Clarissa Carter to say that, but when a hitherto nonpredatory female threw herself into his lap, an explanation had jolly well better be forthcoming, and he started telling her so.

He got no further than an "I say," when to his surprise she put her arms around his neck and said, "Not another word, Marcus. Just put your arms around me, and I will do the rest."

"You will, eh?" he said, pulling away—at the same time thinking that she really did look marvelous in the dotted Swiss, and the subtle scent she was wearing smelled absolutely heavenly.

He was rudely awakened when she said, "You leave me no choice," grabbed him by the hair and, pulling him close, planted her lips firmly on his mouth.

He pushed her away. "You disappoint me, Clarissa. I thought you were above such scheming."

"Scheming?" she said, her voice filled with scorn. "Sir, you flatter yourself." Without more ado, she pressed her lips to his once more.

He pulled back. "You have never kissed a man before, have you?"

"No. I cannot say as I have."

"At least let me show you how," said Marcus, thinking to scare some sense into her.

He pulled her close and kissed her. It was an audacious kiss, probing and coaxing. He fully expected her to jump off his lap and bolt out of the room like a frightened rabbit. Instead, she mewled like a kitten and parted her lips to receive his.

Seeking to discourage her, Marcus deepened the kiss. This was his undoing, for he became lost in her sweet essence. Unwilling for it to end, he made it long and lingering.

His passion receded when the door flew open and to the sound of ripping cloth, Rowena Arden rushed in screaming, "Help! Help! I am undone!"

Her father followed right on her heels, bellowing, "Unhand my daughter, you dastard!" He stopped in his tracks and joined his daughter in openmouthed surprise at seeing Clarissa sitting on the intended victim's knee. A moment later, Mrs. Arden and William piled into him, causing him to stagger.

Clarissa smiled sweetly at the four of them, and then

singled out Rowena. "If you wish to be undone by Lord Fairfax, madam, I am afraid you will have to wait your turn. He is rather busy at the present."

Chagrined, Mr. Arden turned to his wife and pompously intoned, "Mrs. Arden, we must pack our bags and depart this den of evil. I will not have our daughter sullied by such vile behavior."

With noses stuck in the air and chests puffed out, the Ardens filed out of the library like outraged pouter pigeons.

As the door slammed behind them, Clarissa sprang up from his lap.

"It is a good thing you moved, young lady," he snapped. "I was about to deposit you on the carpet." He rose from the chair and, wagging a finger at her, said, "Just what did you think to accomplish by staging that cozy little scene?"

Her eyes flared. "I thought to save your life, though at the moment I cannot imagine why."

"I am perfectly capable of taking care of myself, thank you very much. You have developed into a terrible busybody, and it has to stop."

Clarissa's lower lip quivered. "But Mr. Thistlethwaite said that no one could go against Mr. Arden and win. Then I overheard Mr. Arden say that if you refused to marry his sister he would call you out."

"Did he now?"

"Yes. He thought it a good way to persuade you to marry Miss Arden. But I knew you would rather die than be coerced in such a fashion."

Marcus glowered. "You overstep yourself, Clarissa. How dare you presume to know what I would or would not be willing to die for?"

"I am sorry. In my eagerness to keep you out of a pickle, I suppose I did overstep myself. I assure you, it will not happen again."

Marcus put his hand to his forehead. "You foolish girl, you did not help in the least. You merely pulled me out of one pickle to land me in another."

Clarissa's eyes grew wide. "What do you mean?"

"Simply this. It was up to me to decide whether or not I wished to marry Miss Arden. Your interference has left me no choice. On my account, your reputation is in shreds. Thus I am honor bound to marry you."

Clarissa faced him squarely, her eyes sparking with anger. "You have no choice? You are honor bound?" She gestured with her hand. "Go ahead. Marry Miss Arden and get saddled with that family of ninnyhammers. It would serve you right."

"Why, you bad-tempered brat," he said, his jaw tightly clenched. "A man would have to be mad to marry you."

"Fine," Clarissa snapped, dipping him a curtsy out of sheer force of habit.

"Fine," he snapped, bowing in return.

They marched together through the massive library door and stormed down the hall in opposite directions.

Chapter 20

Without waiting to be told, Clarissa went to her room and started packing her valise. Due to Lady Fairfax's generosity, she had far more clothes than she had arrived with and could not cram them all in.

"I suppose I can get a sack from below stairs," she muttered. "Although since I am not likely to be invited anywhere, I will have little use for most of the clothes, certainly not the ball gowns." She broke into a sob. "I will be lucky if Mama and Papa do not see fit to turn me out into the street."

She was about to throw herself onto her bed and burst into a full-blown crying fit when she was held in check by a rap on the door. She dried her eyes on her sleeve and, trying hard to keep the tremor out of her voice, called out, "Please enter."

Lady Fairfax came in. She glanced at the valise and sighed. "I am so sorry, Clarissa, but it cannot be helped. You should have allowed my son to solve his own problems. We both should have. It is unfortunate that one has to learn the hard way."

"I could not let that brute kill him."

"No, I suppose not. Love is a form of madness, you know. It is inclined to take away one's instinct for self-preservation. I most likely would have done the same for his father, had the situation arisen."

Clarissa felt her stomach lurch. "How did you know that I love him?"

Lady Fairfax laughed, "Dear heavens, child, given enough time, even a blind man would realize that. When you mention his name, it trips off your tongue like a caress. When he enters the room, you catch your breath. Need I go on?"

"No. You must think it a terrible presumption on my part,

but it was not my intention to fall in love with him."

"Of course not. Tell me, Clarissa, why did you reject his offer of marriage?"

Clarissa bit her lip. "He offered because he felt obligated to do so. There was no mention of love."

"And you were too honorable to take advantage of the situation? La, child, you could teach many a daughter of the *ton* the true meaning of nobility. And now there is nothing for it but I should lose you. You have no idea how sad that makes me."

"I also feel sad. I shall miss our afternoons in the sewing room, and I dread having to face my parents. They will be absolutely mortified by the scandal."

"Perhaps it will not be as bad as you think. Of course, your father has to be told the reason for sending you home. Even though you meant well, he will realize that it is no longer proper for you to stay under the same roof as my son. Also, your cause will be helped when he learns that knowledge of this incident will go no further."

Clarissa's eyes widened. "How can that be? The Ardens are bound to give their version of what took place, no doubt depicting his lordship and me in the worst possible light."

"I think not. They have nothing to gain by repeating the story, especially since he—incidentally, it is prudent of you to revert to his honorific—has threatened to expose their sordid little scheme should the slightest hint of scandal be attached to your name."

To Clarissa's surprise, her father was more interested in protecting her than subjecting her to any castigation, but she was dismayed by the way he went about it. His solution was to put as much distance as possible between her and the Earl of Fairfax. To this end, he made arrangements for her to return to his brother Henry's house in Derbyshire.

Marcus left for Brighton at the end of the week, directly after the last carriage bearing guests passed through the gatehouse arch. He had expected to meet with the prince regent in London, but received word that redirected him to Brighton.

He would learn on his arrival that His Royal Highness, tired of receiving the stream of visiting foreign royalty that had poured into London all summer, sought respite at his beloved Pavilion.

It so happened that the prince was still brooding over the snub Alexander, tsar of Russia, had delivered him back in June by refusing to attend the lavish banquet at Carlton House he had prepared for his benefit.

During the ride to Brighton, oblivious to the dissatisfactions plaguing the prince, Marcus was assailed by a feeling of unease regarding his own situation. To put it bluntly, he was not feeling very proud of himself.

On the one hand, he was relieved that Clarissa had made it easy for him to wriggle out of marrying her, but on the other hand, felt less than noble for not having couched his offer in terms that her pride would have allowed her to accept.

When ushered into the presence of His Royal Highness, Marcus found him poring over a set of plans, a troubled look on his face. They exchanged greetings, and then the prince waved Marcus into the seat next to his.

"I am in a dilemma, old chap. I thought this façade would suit, but now I realize it lacks a certain something. What do you think?"

Most of the things that caught the prince's fancy were far too exotic for Marcus's taste, but it was not the thing to admit to the heir to the throne. Marcus thought a moment before replying. "If you entertain the slightest doubt about the plan, sire, you will never be happy with the result. I suggest you look further for your architect."

"Um, yes, I suppose. Dash it all, Fairfax, it is so damned frustrating. Whom do you suggest?"

"I hesitate to recommend anyone, sire. I doubt any can match your vision, but I believe that John Nash might come close. He is highly regarded in certain circles."

The prince regent visibly brightened. "Nash. Of *course*. He quite slipped my mind."

The following week, Marcus prowled around the Pavilion

like a restless cat, the kiss he had shared with Clarissa lingering in his memory. Thoughts of her enigmatic smile paired with the alluring little dimple were just as disturbing. The image popped into his head at the most inappropriate times, filling him with a yearning that was completely alien to him.

Tired of pacing within the confines of the Pavilion grounds, Marcus ventured outside one afternoon and turned onto the Marine Parade with its neat row of houses, all with bow windows gleaming in the afternoon sun.

"I must be mad," he muttered as he settled into an easy stride. "Clarissa is an annoying, interfering busybody. There are times I would like to wring her—" The adjectives beautiful and graceful popped into his mind, stopping him in his tracks.

He was greatly relieved at this point to see Celeste Markham, parasol in hand, coming from the opposite direction.

Thank heavens, he thought *I can do with the distraction.*

"Ah, *cherie,*" she said when they finally met. "Fancy meeting you. Here to hold Prinny's hand, I presume?"

Marcus bowed. "In a manner of speaking. By Jove, Celeste, you look absolutely radiant. You must be in love."

"Must I?" she replied, looking very coy beneath the shade of her cream-colored parasol. "Walk with me, Marcus. I am in somewhat of a quandary and would like your advice."

Marcus got in step with her and waited for her to say something. Finally, he broke the silence. "By any chance, would this quandary of yours involve a certain Mr. Aubrey Sinclair?"

She stopped walking. "Yes, it would. But how would you know that? Has there been gossip concerning us?"

"Not to my knowledge."

Celeste resumed walking, inclining her head to a passerby as she did. "How did you find out about our friendship?"

"I saw the start of it the night of my parents' ball. Sinclair is a capital fellow, and I hoped something would come of it."

"And now he has asked me to marry him and I do not know what to do."

"Do you love him?"

"Madly."

"Then marry the man. Lord knows, you deserve a little happiness."

"It is not quite that simple, and you know it. It is not quite the thing for dowager countesses to remarry. People will talk."

"Let them. The approval of others will not keep you warm on a winter's night."

Celeste looked arch. "A point well taken. Now that we have settled my problem, shall we work on yours?"

"I have no problem."

"How quick you are to deny it. You have a problem, my friend. You look positively harrowed." Her voice gentled. "Do not hold back, Marcus. Perhaps I can help you."

He felt doubtful. "You will think me mad."

"No matter. We are friends. You could foam at the mouth, and I would not judge you."

"It is Clarissa Carter. You discuss the possibility of my foaming at the mouth. I am firmly of the opinion that she has the ability to drive me right round the bend."

Celeste stopped at the summer house belonging to her family. "Come, we shall take tea while you tell me all about it."

By their second cup, Marcus had concluded his story.

Celeste looked very thoughtful. "You say she drives you wild and there are times you would like to strangle her?"

Marcus nodded.

"Can you think of any other girl who affects you this way?"

"I should hope not. One is enough."

Celeste patted his hand. "It must be maddening when she interferes in your affairs, constantly trying to save you from God knows what, you say?"

Marcus nodded.

"Well, that establishes one thing."

"And that is?"

"Your Clarissa is in love with you. But I realized that the night I saw you together at the ball. She is not very good at hiding her feelings."

Marcus put his cup and saucer on the table. "That is preposterous."

"You think so? For your sake, I hope not."

"Celeste, what exactly are you implying?"

"That you are absolutely, positively in love with this girl."

"Absolutely?"

"Positively."

"That cannot be." Marcus ran his hands through his hair, got up, and started to pace the floor. "I thought being in love would feel glorious. I feel downright wretched."

"That is because you are resisting the idea. Once you give in to it, Marcus, you will find that being in love is the most glorious feeling in the world."

He stopped pacing. "Are you sure about that?"

"Absolutely and positively," she said sweetly.

Marcus bowed. And headed for the door.

Chapter 21

Lady Fairfax looked up in surprise when Marcus burst into the dining room unannounced. "Good heavens, you look all in a lather. Is there something amiss? Percy? Is he all right?" she asked.

"Relax, Mother, your lamb is fine."

"Then what possible reason could you have for arriving at this time of night looking as if your horse rode *you* instead of the other way around?"

"The best of all possible reasons, Mother. I am in love."

"And this girl—she loves you back?"

"Celeste Markham seems to think so."

Lady Fairfax bolted out of her chair. "Celeste Markham is behind this? I might have known. Marcus, Marcus, what light skirt has you in her coil?"

"Perhaps you will not approve of my choice in a bride, but I assure you, she is by no means a light skirt Mother, it is your precious Clarissa who has stolen my heart."

Lady Fairfax touched her throat "Clarissa? Oh, Marcus, you have no idea how happy that makes me."

"Really, now? *You* have no idea how happy *that* makes *me*. I thought to ask her first thing tomorrow morning."

"That will not be possible. The Carters have taken her to stay with his brother in Derbyshire."

"What on earth for?"

Lady Fair smiled impishly. "To keep her out of your evil clutches, apparently."

"Of all the nerve. No matter, I will talk to Carter in the morning and find out just *where* in Derbyshire. I will not rest until this is settled."

"Alas, Marcus, that will not be possible. It will be another three days before the Carters return."

"I do not wish to wait another three days. I want to see Clarissa as soon as possible."

"Good heavens, Marcus, you have spent all these years avoiding marriage, and now you cannot wait another three days?"

"I know it's mad. It does not make sense to me either, but I have this feeling that I have not a moment to lose."

"In that case, I suppose I should tell you where she is."

Marcus gave her a look. "Please *do*."

"Very well. The Henry Carters live at Oakwood, a manor house directly south of a village called Stoney Middleton. How you find it is up to you, dear."

It was still dark when Marcus and a burly groom named Bart set out for Derbyshire, both riding powerful bay geldings with equally stalwart chestnuts in tow to share the burden of getting them there. Taking Bart along had been his mother's idea.

Covering more than half the distance that day, they stayed over at an inn and reached Stoney Middleton the following afternoon. When Marcus called at Oakwood, he was surprised to discover that it was a fine Elizabethan structure set in well-maintained grounds. It would seem that Henry Carter was very plump in the pocket.

A young maid answered the door. To his dismay, she told him that Miss Clarissa Carter had left with the rest of the family to spend some time in London.

"Mr. Carter could've saved himself the trouble of bringing her all this way. My goodness, what a trip. I've never been any farther than the next village my whole life. She was only here for three days when the master took it into his head to gather up the lot of 'em and leave for London."

"Might I inquire as to where they are staying in London?"

"I am sorry, your lordship, but I warn't told. Our Mr. Jones could tell you, but he's gone to visit his mum. Proper plagued by rheumatics she is."

"Damn," Marcus muttered under his breath as he rode away. "Now I have to return to Fairfax to discover her whereabouts."

On reaching Fairfax village, Marcus went straight to the Carter house.

Mr. Carter responded to his knock. As they faced each other in the doorway, the steward's spine stiffened slightly. "Good evening, your lordship, is there anything I can do for you?" he asked, his tone lacking its usual cordiality.

"Good evening. I have just come from Derbyshire. I should have waited for you to return and saved myself the trouble. Mr. Carter, I am looking for Clarissa. I understand she is with your brother in London."

Mr. Carter shook his head, "I will not lift a finger to help you. Good heavens, man, what do you want of us? You besmirched my little girl's name. Her mother and I have been deprived of her company. We have had enough. Leave her be, I beg of you."

"Forgive me. In my haste I forgot to explain." Marcus took a deep breath. "Mr. Carter, I want to *marry* Clarissa, not dishonor her. I humbly beg your permission to pay her court. And to this end, I would like to see her as soon as possible."

Mr. Carter seemed to wrestle with these words before answering. Finally, he said. "Very well. You have never given me reason to doubt your word. Please come inside while I get the direction for you."

"Mr. Carter, I would rather not. I have ridden hard, and do not smell too sweet. I neither wish to sully your parlor nor offend your wife's sensibilities with my presence."

"As you wish." Mr. Carter returned shortly with the Bloomsbury address. "My brother has rented it for a few weeks. Wants his wife to enjoy the city entertainments."

As soon as Marcus rode away, Mr. Carter surprised his wife by getting down on his knees and saying, "I am begging your pardon, my dear. You were right and I was wrong. Staying at Fairfax Towers did afford our daughter a brilliant match."

She shook with excitement. "Let me guess. That nice Mr. Thistlethwaite has offered for her."

"Sorry, my dear. You will have to make do with an earl for a son-in-law."

"You mean *our* earl? My dearest Edwin, it is a mother's

dream come true." A look of unholy glee crossed her face. "Wait till those Cobbett twins find out. It will teach those little cats to call our daughter names."

"Is it all right for me to get up now? My knees are killing me."

Mrs. Carter kissed the top of his head and helped him to his feet.

When Marcus finally reached home, he apprised his mother of his plans for the following day, then soaked in a hot bath and, too tired to eat, collapsed in his bed. To his chagrin, he did not waken until almost ten o'clock the following morning. By eleven, he was mounted on Achilles and on his way to London.

He stopped at Doctor's Commons first and purchased a special marriage license, then found his way to the address in Bloomsbury. It turned out to be a tall, narrow house, with three stories rising above the ground floor. As he knocked on the door, a church clock struck six.

A portly butler answered the door. Marcus handed the man his card and asked to see Miss Clarissa Carter.

The butler shook his head. "The family is attending a Grand Masque at the Vauxhall Gardens as the guests of Lord Gravewood." The man preened. "Of course, you know, his lordship sent his own carriage for the master's family. He has honored Miss Clarissa with his attentions, and as a consequence, has extended his gracious compliments toward the whole family."

Marcus felt gutted. It was not the fact that he had a rival that upset him so much as the character of his rival.

Lord Gravewood was known to be a cruel, mean-spirited creature whose company was shunned by more discerning members of the *ton*. His lordship had married and buried two wives. Rumor had it that both had received cruel treatment at his hands. Of a certainty, both died under suspicious circumstances, his first wife supposedly falling down a flight of stairs, the second drowning in a lake on his estate.

Shaken by what he had learned, Marcus rode to the family house in Mayfair. As he walked through the door, he could hear the murmur of voices coming from the withdrawing room. He poked his head around the door to find his mother engaged in an animated conversation with Mr. and Mrs. Carter and Mr. Halliwell, the vicar of St. Martin's and joined them.

"Ah. I see you had no difficulty in organizing this get-together, Mother. Mr. and Mrs. Carter, Mr. Halliwell, I am glad you could come at such short notice. Hope the journey was not too uncomfortable."

"Not at all, your lordship," Mrs. Carter said. "Your Berline is so well sprung."

"I am told you intend to marry Miss Carter this evening," the Reverend Halliwell inserted.

"That is if I can find her. Mr. Carter's brother has taken her to a Grand Masque at Vauxhall. I shall do my utmost to find them. In the meantime, I leave you all in my mother's capable hands."

Marcus rang for the butler and asked him to see that the Berline was again made ready for use. He then repaired to his room and emerged half an hour later dressed for an evening out, looking the better for Hillman's ministrations.

Marcus scoured the grottoes and walkways of Vauxhall Gardens for an hour and a half without encountering either Clarissa or Lord Gravewood.

He did not expect to run into any of the other Carters, certain that her uncle had deliberately left Clarissa to the tender mercies of Lord Gravewood, who was no doubt planning to seduce, or worse, defile Clarissa with a view to forcing her into marriage. In which case what better place than Vauxhall, where the screams of an innocent young girl could easily be mistaken for those of a bawd taking her pleasure?

He scoured the notorious Dark Walk one more time, running the gauntlet of drunken roués and their half-naked Cyprians as they staggered into the shadows, but to no avail. He decided to return to his carriage and go back to Bloomsbury. He did not care if he had to wake up Henry Carter's whole household. He had to make certain Clarissa was safe.

If it is otherwise, Carter and Gravewood had better be prepared to meet their Maker, he thought grimly.

He hurried to the line of parked carriages being guarded by grooms waiting for their masters to return. He reached there to find Grimes standing behind the Berline talking to one of the other grooms. He had the carriage door open before Grimes even realized he had returned. The groom quickly took his place at the reins, looking a little disconcerted for being remiss in his duty.

Marcus bent down to get into the carriage and realized there was a female sitting on the rear seat. She had on a voluminous black cloak with the hood pulled over her forehead. Where it left off, a black domino began, leaving the upper half of her face hidden.

No, not another one! Wonderful!

He pulled back out of the carriage and glared at his driver. "I swear, if you let one more lovesick female get by you, Grimes, you and I are going to part company."

"Criminy, your lordship. She must move like a cat. I never 'eard a thing."

Marcus stuck his head into the carriage once more. "I will thank you to remove your person from my carriage, young lady. I am not in the mood to listen to any protestations of love that might be forthcoming. Who are you, in any case? Your parents must be frantic wondering where you are."

He pulled off her mask and saw it was Clarissa, blazing mad, the tears running down her cheeks.

"You are mistaken, your lordship. I do not find you the least bit lovable. I came to your carriage to seek sanctuary and as far as I am concerned *you* may go to the devil!" She broke down and sobbed. "Why, oh why, must gentlemen behave so abominably?"

Marcus climbed in beside her, banging his head in the process. Ignoring the pain, he crooned, "There, there."

He took her in his arms, and the hood of her cape slipped back. Her hair gleamed like copper in the dimness of the carriage light. Marcus pushed her away from him just far enough to look into her eyes. "Tell me, Clarissa, did that dastard Gravewood hurt you in anyway?"

Her eyes widened. "How did you find out about him?"

"It is of no consequence, but if he hurt you I will make him pay."

Clarissa looked sheepish. "No. It was the other way around, actually."

Marcus was not too surprised to hear this.

"In the crush, we became separated from my uncle and his family. As we were walking down this Grand Cross Walk, his lordship's attitude toward me became—how shall I put it—amorous. My goodness, the man is almost old enough to be my father's father!"

"The presumptuous cad," Marcus inserted.

"When I rebuffed him, he dropped his pleasant demeanor, and his expression became positively frightening. He then called me a vile name which I do not care to repeat, grabbed my arm, and pulled me toward the bushes."

"How did you get away?"

"I kicked him on the shins and hid until he gave up looking for me."

Marcus pulled a twig from her hair. "Up an elm, perchance?"

She smiled at this. Marcus melted at the sight of the little crescent dimple.

"I could not say for sure, the lighting there was dim," she said, then suddenly clung to him. "Marcus, I was so afraid."

He stroked her hair. "Hush, darling. I will take care of you."

Her lower lip quivered. "You are too kind, Marcus. I feel so ashamed, telling you to go to the devil and all."

He nuzzled her throat. "Clarissa, my sweet, marry me and we shall go to the devil together if it pleases you." He nibbled her earlobe. "Although I can think of a far, far, better place I would rather take you." He gently nipped at her lower lip. "Darling, I am in love with you. Please say you will marry me."

Clarissa entwined her arms around his neck and kissed him. "I love you more."

Suddenly Grimes rapped on the roof. "Need a little help getting rid of this one, milord?"

Marcus kissed Clarissa on the nose. "No, thank you, Grimes. This one I have decided to keep."

The Dowager's Daughter

Affairs of the state will soon give way to affairs of the heart.

Althea Markham shoulders many burdens of being an unattached countess—wading through the collection of gold-diggers and rogues to find a suitable husband, providing her family with a male hair, and most of all, protecting her mother, who tends to acts more debutante than dowager. As she sneaks away for illicit meetings with a mysterious stranger, Althea is determined to unveil his identity—and his intentions.

Desperate to escape from beneath the shadow of his older brother, John Ridley takes part in a daring game of espionage against the French. Posing as a smuggler, he engages with the charming Celeste Markham. But despite her winsome allure, it is her daughter, Althea, who seizes John's attention.

As affairs of the state give way to affairs of heart, John must convince Althea that she can trust him with her future, and her love.

Educating Emily

He taught her the ways of the world, and she taught him the ways of love.

Fated to be sold into a loveless marriage, Emily Walsingham runs away. But when she is rescued by dashing James Garwood, she fall desperately in love. Recognized by James's mother, Emily is declared the perfect wife for him, despite the fact that he has yet to declare his love for her.

When James Garwood agrees to marry Emily, he never expected to be any more than a tolerable companion. But as she proves to be more caring and intelligent than he imagined, a man thought to be incapable of true devotion will learn more than he bargained for about falling in love.

A Kiss For Lucy

Could the wrong woman be the right love?

Rescued from a life of hardship by her wealthy uncle, Lucy Garwood can't escape the shadow of her elitist relatives. She longs to be loved and respected in her own right, but it seems that as an orphan, her place amongst her blueblood family is unlikely to improve—that is until a case of mistaken identity leads to a kiss from a dashing stranger…

Robert Renquist, Duke of Lindorough, is determined to win the heart of the lovely Maude. But in an attempt to sweep her off of her feet with a daring act of passion, it isn't Maude he kisses, but her half-niece instead. Though conscious of his standing in society, Robert can't deny his unmistakable attraction to Lucy, and he'll soon discover there is only one thing more powerful than his noble lineage—love.

Printed in the USA
CPSIA information can be obtained
at www.ICGtesting.com
JSHW031714140824
68134JS00038B/3683

9 781626 816817